Sweets & Treats

ALSO BY BARBARA HINSKE

Available at Amazon in Print, Audio, and for Kindle

The Rosemont Series

Coming to Rosemont

Weaving the Strands

Uncovering Secrets

Drawing Close

Bringing Them Home

Shelving Doubts

Restoring What Was Lost

No Matter How Far

When Dreams There Be

Novellas

The Night Train

The Christmas Club (adapted for The Hallmark Channel, 2019)

Paws & Pastries

Sweets & Treats

Snowflakes, Cupcakes & Kittens

Workout Wishes & Valentine Kisses

Wishes of Home

Novels in the Guiding Emily Series

Guiding Emily

The Unexpected Path

Over Every Hurdle

Down the Aisle

Novels in the "Who's There?!" Collection

Deadly Parcel

Final Circuit

CONNECT WITH BARBARA HINSKE ONLINE

Sign up for her newsletter at **BarbaraHinske.com**
    Goodreads.com/BarbaraHinske
    Facebook.com/BHinske
    Instagram/barbarahinskeauthor
    TikTok.com/BarbaraHinske
    Pinterest.com/BarbaraHinske
    Twitter.com/BarbaraHinske
    Search for **Barbara Hinske on YouTube**
    bhinske@gmail.com

SWEETS & TREATS
BOOK 2 IN THE PAWS & PASTRIES SERIES

BARBARA HINSKE

CASA DEL NORTHERN PUBLISHING

This book may not be reproduced in whole or in part without written permission of the author, with the exception of brief quotations within book reviews or articles. This book is a work of fiction. Any resemblance to actual persons, living or dead, or places or events is coincidental.

Copyright © 2022 Barbara Hinske.

Cover by Elizabeth Mackey, Copyright © 2022.

All rights reserved.

ISBN: 978-1-7349249-78

Library of Congress Control Number: 2022903081

Casa del Northern Publishing

Phoenix, Arizona

❦ Created with Vellum

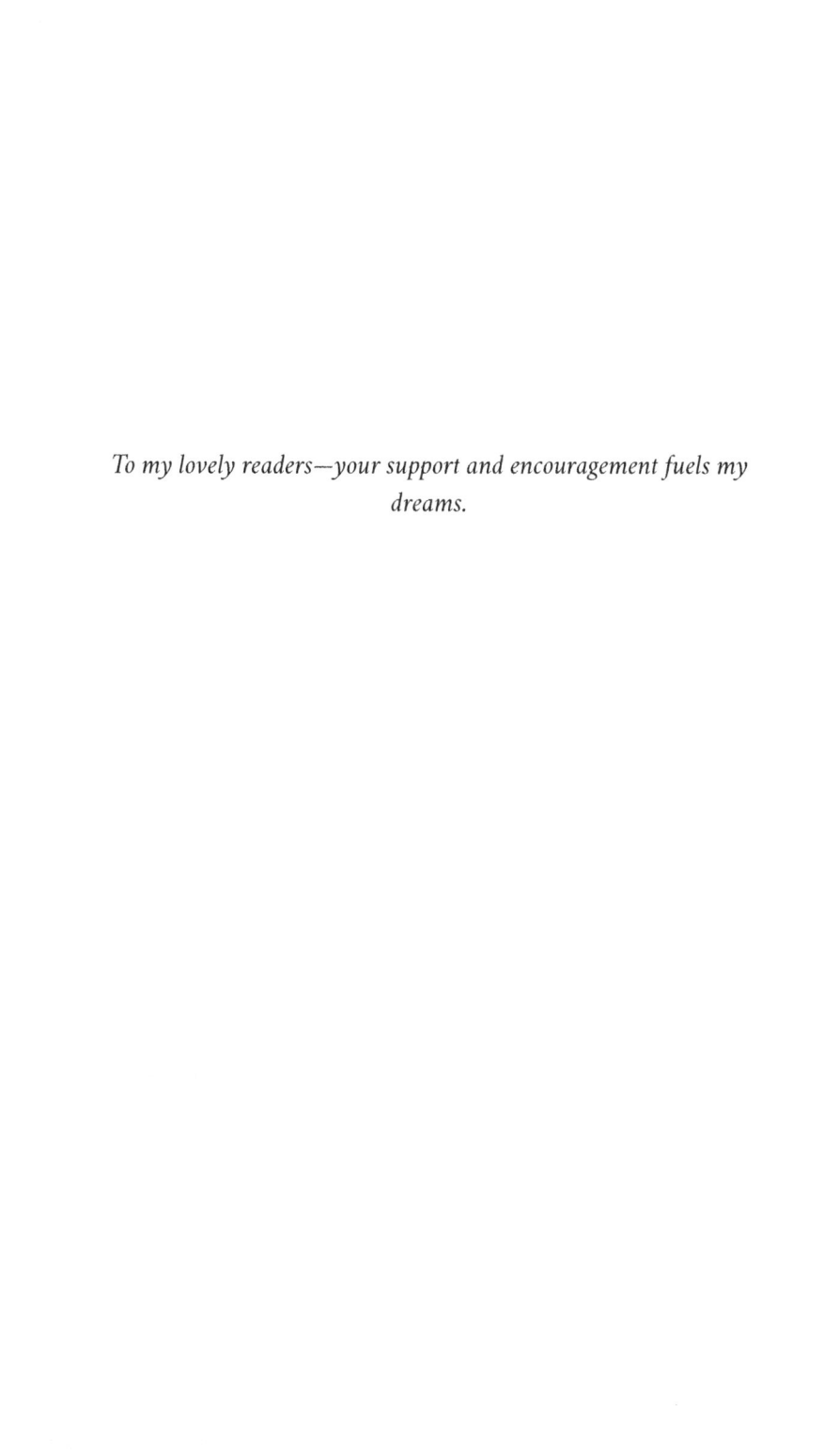

To my lovely readers—your support and encouragement fuels my dreams.

CHAPTER 1

Clara Conway pulled her chestnut curls out of the collar of her heavy coat and arranged them around her shoulders. She swiped lip gloss across her lips. It was time to head to the lobby of the Pinewood Springs Motel.

"Come, Noelle," she said as the terrier dachshund mix sprang off the bed and ran to Clara. "You know your name already, don't you, girl?" Clara cooed as she bent to snap a leash on the squirming animal. "Hold still," Clara said as Noelle wagged her tail so hard, she almost knocked herself to the ground.

"There." Clara secured the leash in place and stood. "We're going to Maisie and Josef's for Christmas dinner. You're going to love them. In fact, Josef's the reason that you and I met. Kurt's picking us up."

The couple made their way to the lobby, the stiletto heels on Clara's boots tapping the sidewalk while Noelle inspected every bush along their path. Clara checked her watch. They were five minutes early. The calm, sunny afternoon was pleasant, even though the temperature was below freezing.

Clara inhaled the crisp air slowly and wondered, for the umpteenth time, if she was doing the right thing. Everything seemed to be falling into place for her. Didn't they always say that, if something was meant to be, it would be easy? That you shouldn't have to force things—like pounding a square peg into a round hole? Surely her dream of owning a successful patisserie-style bakery was a worthy goal. She loved food and had worked with it her whole life.

She'd become a dietician to have a viable career involving food, but she'd never loved her studies or any of her professional positions using her degree. Clara had wanted to own a bakery since she'd learned to bake at her mother's side all those years ago. Now that she'd inherited the necessary funds from her mother—together with a note insisting she use the money to accomplish her dream—she had to be on the right path.

Clara shook her head and groaned. Her thoughts were driving her crazy. She'd decided to open a patisserie here in Pinewood—in an available space she'd seen only hours earlier.

Noelle looked back at her new mistress and came to her side, sitting at Clara's feet.

Clara stooped and rubbed along the strip of brown fur that ran the length of Noelle's mostly white body. "Kurt is going to be our landlord and we'll get more details when we meet with him tomorrow afternoon, won't we? I need to relax and quit thinking about it."

Noelle gave Clara's hand a quick lick.

Clara chuckled and kissed the top of Noelle's head. She stood, fishing her phone out of her purse. She'd distract herself by checking her email. She'd been so busy churning out baked goods for Johanson's Diner that she hadn't checked her account in days. She usually only received spam that she didn't want or postings from food bloggers that she followed. There was nothing urgent about any of that.

Clara was scrolling through her inbox when her finger froze over the screen. There was an email from her attorney with a one-word subject line: *Update.* He'd emailed early the prior morning.

The sun went behind a cloud and Clara shivered. She'd thought that Tom had planned to take the week off. What was so important that he had contacted her on Christmas Eve? Tom had assured her that the judge would dismiss her husband's motion questioning her mental competence in the divorce action she'd filed against Travis. Tom had told her that Travis's motion was a stall tactic to delay the proceedings and the judge would see through it.

Surely Tom was letting her know everything had gone as planned. She tapped the screen and opened his email. The message was brief.

Urgent. Please call.

Clara swallowed hard, the acid pooling at the back of her throat making her breath sour. *What in the world? Could something have gone wrong?*

Clara pulled her eyes from the screen to see Kurt's car turn into the motel's driveway. Whatever Tom had to tell her would have to wait until tomorrow. She couldn't call him now.

Clara's eyes stung with sudden tears. Travis still had the power to ruin everything. She shoved her phone back into her purse and fished around for a breath mint. She popped it into her mouth and crunched it as Kurt pulled up to her.

Clara forced a smile onto her lips as she opened the rear passenger door for Noelle and then slipped into the front seat.

The tall, almost-handsome man who was one of her only

friends in Pinewood grinned at her. "Are you ready for one of the best meals you'll ever have?"

Clara stiffened her spine. She would not let anything Travis had—or had not—done spoil this day. Travis Conway no longer controlled her happiness or her destiny. "I most certainly am," Clara said. She and her attorney would handle whatever nonsense he had come up with. Clara relaxed into her seat, telling herself that everything was going to be fine.

* * *

CLARA TOOK the dinner plate from Kurt, dried it, and set it on top of the stack of clean plates.

"I think that's it," Kurt said, sweeping his gaze over the kitchen counters. The chaos of dirty pots, pans, dishes, and cutlery had been cleared and cleaned. A three-wick balsam candle burned on the island, its soft woodsy scent permeating the kitchen. "We got through these dishes in record time. Thank you for helping."

"Of course," Clara said. "I completely agree with you that anyone who cooks—or hosts—a big meal like this shouldn't also do the cleanup." She folded her dishtowel and laid it next to the sink. "You were right—that meal was fabulous. The rib roast was perfectly seasoned and you could cut it with a fork."

"Wait until you try this white chocolate raspberry cheesecake," Kurt said, pointing to the elegant dessert on a cut crystal cake stand. "I mean..." he stammered, "I know you're a baker and everything, but this is really something." He cut his eyes to hers.

Clara put her hand on Kurt's elbow. "The very best bakers appreciate the successes of others. Maybe that's one reason I enjoy the field so much. Bakers are a collegial bunch. And there are thousands of different baked goods from all over the world—no one can be an expert at everything."

Kurt smiled at her. "Maisie has dessert plates, forks, and coffee cups on the buffet in the dining room. As soon as the coffee finishes brewing, we'll take it and the cake into the dining room."

"Sounds like a plan."

"Do you still want to tell Maisie and Josef about your decision to stay in Pinewood and open a patisserie?"

Clara looked away from him.

"Having second thoughts?"

"Why would you think that?"

"I don't know," he said slowly, "but your mood seems different from when we ran into each other this morning in front of the vacant space I own. You were so excited about renting it for the patisserie you said you've wanted to open since you were a kid. You were—I don't know how to describe it—bubbling with energy." He raked his fingers through his hair. "And now you seem… so subdued." He leaned around her to catch her eye. "You don't have to go through with this, you know."

Clara took a deep breath and swallowed hard. She would not let that stupid email from her attorney rob her of her self-confidence. "No. No second thoughts. I've just been waiting for the right moment to bring it up."

"Then I think dessert will be the perfect time," he said as the last drop of coffee dripped into the pot. Kurt removed it from the dispenser.

Clara squared her shoulders, picked up the cake stand, and the two young people entered the dining room where Maisie and Josef were chatting amiably with her sister and brother-in-law.

All eyes locked on the cake stand that Clara placed in the middle of the table. Conversation ceased.

Maisie pushed her blond hair, streaked with gray, out of her eyes and leaned across Josef to grin at Sarah. Her blue eyes sparkled. "It looks amazing—as always."

Sarah flushed with pleasure. "I make the same thing every year. I'm surprised you don't get tired of it."

"Never!" Kurt said.

"Would you do the honors, dear?" Sarah said to Clara.

Clara nodded, and Josef passed her a stack of dessert plates. "It's so pretty," Clara said. "It's almost a shame to cut into it." She cut her eyes to Kurt. "Almost." Clara picked up the cake knife and began slicing and plating servings of the delectable treat. She passed the plates around the table as the diners picked up their forks, eager to begin.

* * *

"You've done it again, Sarah," Kurt said, putting down his fork. "That was absolutely delicious."

"I second that," Josef said, patting his stomach. Short and stocky, he watched what he ate. "Now that I'm a senior citizen, I can't eat like I did when I was Kurt's age. I shouldn't have had such a large piece, but it was worth every calorie."

Sarah beamed. "I'm so glad you enjoyed it. I know it's your favorite. And I'm sending all the leftovers home with you, Kurt."

"I can't hog it all," Kurt said. He addressed Don. "You'll want more of this."

"I love my wife's cooking, but my cardiologist says I can only have one piece. I'm better off if I don't have to resist temptation. You'll be doing me a favor."

"If you're sure…" Kurt said.

"Enjoy it while you can, son. I could eat like that when I was your age, but not anymore."

"Then I'll gladly take it home. Thank you."

Conversation lulled as everyone savored their coffee. The grandfather clock in the hallway chimed the half-hour.

Kurt caught Clara's eye and cocked an eyebrow.

Clara nodded and cleared her throat. "This was a magnificent meal," she said. "Start to finish. Thank you for inviting me."

"We've loved having you here," Josef said. "We'll always be grateful to you for stepping in like you did at the diner."

"You've made me feel so welcome here," Clara said, her voice cracking.

"That's because you are welcome," Maisie broke in. "We're extremely fond of you. We'll be sorry to see you go." She pulled a tissue out of the pocket of her cardigan and dabbed at her eyes. "I can hardly stand to think about it."

"There's something I'd like to say about that," Clara said. "Let me start out by saying that if you don't want me to do this—if you have any reservations whatsoever—I won't. All you have to do is say the word." She leaned her elbows on the table and looked from Josef to Maisie.

They glanced at each other and turned their attention back to Clara.

"I've decided that I'd like to stay in Pinewood and open my own patisserie. It's been my dream. When my car broke down in Pinewood, I was looking for the right place to settle. I wasn't planning on Pinewood, but it seems fate placed me here." She looked into their kind eyes and continued in a rush. "I have the skill and the capital to start a bakery. And when Noelle and I were exploring the downtown area this morning,

I found the perfect location—which happens to be owned by Kurt."

Josef's eyes twinkled as he turned them on Kurt.

Kurt shrugged.

"What do you think?" Clara asked. "I don't want to be your competition. I know you sell a lot of baked goods from the diner, and I don't want to take any business away from you. You've been so kind to me, and I'd hate for you to think that I was using you to establish my reputation in town as a baker and then I up and…"

Josef held up a hand to stop her. "You've done no such thing. You've earned that reputation with those remarkable Christmas cookies you made that were the talk of the town." He leaned toward his wife until their shoulders touched.

She nodded and patted his shoulder, signaling her unspoken approval to something she knew he wanted to say.

Josef straightened. "Maisie and I have come to the conclusion that we're closing the bakery operation at the diner as of the first of the year. It's simply too much for us to keep up with."

Maisie lifted her chin. "I've loved working with you in the bakery, Clara, but I'm still not one hundred percent after my stroke and I can't manage the bakery operation anymore. I hate to give up, but we have to. We're going to buy our baked goods for the diner from a commercial operation." She sighed heavily. "It'll be the end of an era."

Josef turned to Maisie, his head nodding in excitement. "Why don't we buy what we need from Clara? She'll produce the quality we need. She already knows what we require on a daily basis and has worked with our staff on most of it."

Maisie looked up at him and grinned. "That'll make me feel so much better about backing away."

The couple looked at Clara. "What do you say? Can we be your first standing customer?"

Clara glanced at Kurt, who was nodding in satisfaction. He'd told her he thought this might happen when he'd encountered her with her face pressed against the plate-glass window of the vacant space, earlier that day.

"That would be incredible," Clara said. "Supplying the diner would set me up for success from the get-go." She rocked back in her chair. "Are you really sure you don't mind?"

"It'd be the answer to my prayers, to have you stay here," Maisie said, dabbing again at her eyes.

"You'll need permits and licenses, equipment and fixtures, before you can begin," Josef said. "Why don't you run your baking operation out of the bakery building behind the diner until you get all that set up? We eventually plan to sell the building to the Pinewood Springs Motel. They've been offering to buy it from us for years. The motel wants to turn it into a fitness center. They claim they get a lot of requests for one."

"What are you going to do with your equipment and fixtures?" Clara asked.

"Sell it." Josef looked at her. "To you if you want it. I'll give you a good price."

"We'll have it professionally appraised and I'll buy it all at full value," Clara said.

Josef started to protest.

"That's my final offer," Clara said.

"Okay," Josef said. "Then it will come with my consulting services. I can help you with all the required permits. I'll introduce you to the best suppliers in the area, and I know where you can buy anything else you might need."

"What about the current bakery staff?" Clara asked. "Would they come to work for me?"

"I'm sure they would. Everyone likes you." Maisie clapped her hands together. "I was dreading telling them we were shutting down, and that they'd have to find other jobs. Now I don't have to."

Clara rested her forehead on her hand. "This is all fantastic. Beyond fantastic! Wow—I sure have a lot to do. My first step is to lease that space."

"And form a limited liability company to run the business," Josef chimed in.

Clara swung to Kurt. "Can you help me with that?"

"I most certainly can. We should be able to have your business entity formed by the beginning of the new year. What do you plan to call yourself?"

"Sweets & Treats," she replied. "I've had this name in my head since I was little."

"I'll get the paperwork started in the morning."

Clara's eyes were wide as she looked around the table. "Holy cow. I'm really doing this!"

"Yes, you are," Maisie chuckled. "And now, I think you need to head home and get some sleep. You've got a big day ahead of you."

Clara pushed back her chair. "I'll be at the diner by five to get the day's baking started," she said.

"Don't worry about that," Josef said. "Everyone's at the mall on the day after Christmas. We'll be very slow through New Year's. Take the week off to get yourself started. You've got a lot on your plate."

Everyone rose from the table.

Noelle, who had been lying at Clara's feet under the table, hoping for table scraps, emerged and clung to her mistress.

As coats were donned, and goodbyes were said, Maisie and Clara stepped into the darkened kitchen. Maisie drew Clara into a hug. "This is what I wanted most for Christmas," Maisie whispered into Clara's ear. "That you would stay."

Clara kissed the older woman on her damp cheek, her own tears flowing. "I think we're both getting our wish for Christmas."

CHAPTER 2

Kurt turned off the highway toward the motel.

"Would you mind dropping us off by the diner?" Clara asked.

Kurt glanced at her, his expression quizzical.

"I'm not supposed to have a dog in my room," Clara said. "I've been bringing her over here to do her business—out of sight of the motel."

"Ahhh... That makes sense."

"Originally, I wasn't too worried about breaking the rules, since I only planned to have her with me until the shelter opened up again." Clara stretched her hand through the break between the seats and patted the top of Noelle's head as she paced in the back seat. "Now that I'm keeping Noelle, I'd better keep her a secret until I find a permanent place to live."

Clara brought her hand back to her forehead. "I guess I've got to search for housing, too."

Kurt pulled to a stop in the part of the diner's parking lot hidden from view by the Pinewood Springs Motel.

Clara got out of the car and retrieved Noelle from the back seat.

Kurt exited the driver's side.

"You don't have to get out," Clara said. "Noelle and I can walk to our room from here."

Kurt joined her as she took Noelle to the snow-covered grass. "I'm not going to leave the two of you here."

"We'll be fine. It'll feel good to walk after that huge meal."

"I'm still not leaving you here."

Noelle scented the air, then put her nose to the ground as she searched for the perfect spot.

"I was thinking—why don't we meet at my vacant space at one o'clock tomorrow? You haven't seen the inside yet. You'll want to do that before you commit to a lease."

"I think it's exactly what I want, but that's a good idea."

"If you have second thoughts about the space, there are other locations in town that would fit the bill. And if you get cold feet about opening your patisserie in Pinewood, you can change your mind."

"Neither of those is going to happen, but I'm very anxious to see the place. My mind is whirling with all the possibilities."

Noelle trotted back to them, her bedtime comfort break completed.

Clara turned and took a step back to the parking lot. The heel of her dress boots caught in the stiff, dormant grass, and she teetered.

Kurt caught her before she tumbled to her knees.

Clara grasped his outstretched arms as she extricated her foot and steadied herself.

"Whoa," he said. "I don't know how anyone walks in those things."

Clara smiled up into his face, hidden in shadow. "Stiletto heels aren't very practical—I'll give you that. They just make your legs look great."

"*You* look great, Clara Conway, with or without stiletto heels."

His breath was warm on her face. She wanted to stay there, his arms holding her and their faces close. She wanted Kurt to kiss her.

Clara stepped back as the thought hit her. When was the last time that she'd longed for a man's touch? Travis's inattention and infidelities had annihilated her feelings for him. She hadn't wanted any sort of romance with her soon-to-be ex-husband for months, but she was still legally married, and she shouldn't be dreaming about kissing another man in the moonlight.

Noelle jumped between them and began pulling on the leash.

Kurt dropped his arms to his side, the intimacy broken. "I'll walk the two of you to your door," he said. "And I'll see you at one tomorrow."

* * *

Clara shut the door to her room and leaned her back against it as she removed her gloves. She closed her eyes, remembering the feel of Kurt's hands on her arms, of his face close to hers. She shook her head to dispel the image. What in the world was wrong with her? She was acting like she was in junior high school again, contemplating her first crush. She didn't have time for this sort of foolishness.

Clara moved to the bed and removed her boots. She patted

the spot next to her, but Noelle stayed at her feet, wagging her tail expectantly.

"You want your dinner, don't you, girl?" Clara patted the dog's head. She went to the dresser, spread kibble on a towel on the floor, and stepped out of Noelle's way.

"That'll be at the top of our list," she told the dog, who was happily crunching her food. "You'll need official food and water bowls. Given the weather, you'll also need a sweater. Or two. And a few more toys. You should see a vet, too. I'll need to make sure you've had all your shots."

Clara changed into her flannel pajamas and crawled under the covers, laptop in hand. She stacked up her pillows and nested herself into place with her laptop on her knees.

Noelle finished her supper, took a long drink from the makeshift water bowl, and hopped onto the bed, curling up against Clara.

"I have a food handler's license from working at the diner," she said to the dog, who was drifting off to sleep. "So that's done. And I've been practicing the items I'd offer in my patisserie for years. I know what my menu will be. I've got a vision board packed away in the stuff in the back of my SUV, so I already know what I want my patisserie to look like."

Clara opened her laptop and created a new folder titled "Sweets & Treats." She set up separate files for Legal, Recipes/Menu, Furniture/Fixtures/Equipment, Banking and Finance, and Staffing.

Clara's fingers flew across the keyboard as she created to-do lists of all the things that she needed to accomplish to settle in Pinewood and open her business.

She was working on a spreadsheet for a master list of ingredients, then woke with a start shortly after two o'clock, realizing she'd fallen asleep. Clara saved her work, shut her laptop, and turned out her light. If she was going to be making big decisions later that day, she needed to get some rest.

Noelle stretched and rolled onto her back. Clara pulled the warm animal close and fell asleep.

CHAPTER 3

Maisie pulled up a stool and sat, leaning her elbows on the countertop. She surveyed the familiar scene in front of her. The ten women who had worked for their diner for decades, turning out the signature baked goods they were famous for, were moving around the bakery in a practiced choreography. Next to being a mother, running this bakery was the life accomplishment that Maisie was most proud of.

Now that Rachel—her only child—had passed away three years earlier, the bakery had taken on more significance in her life. She and Josef loved Kurt Holbrook, their son-in-law, like he was their own, but he was a grown man with a busy life. Coming in here every morning, being surrounded by these kind and comforting women, and losing herself in the touch and smell of baking, had saved her sanity during the dark days after Rachel's death and had allowed her to heal. Maisie's eyes stung with unshed tears.

Betty glanced over at Maisie and knew, in that way good

friends do, that something was troubling her. Betty switched off the commercial mixer that was whirring away with the dough for the morning's cinnamon rolls, wiped her floury hands on her apron, and came to stand by her friend.

"How are you doing today, Maisie?" She peered anxiously at her. "I know the holidays are always hard for you. It's impossible not to miss Rachel."

Maisie didn't want to say that she'd soon be stepping away from the bakery altogether—that advancing age and the after-effects of her stroke were forcing this unwelcome change. The thought of telling her crew that she was retiring was only made bearable by knowing that Clara would hire them to bake for the patisserie. These dear women would keep the jobs that they loved, and that she knew they all depended upon. She and Clara would meet with them later in the week, after Clara had her paperwork in order.

Maisie pushed herself to her feet. There was no point sitting here, wallowing in self-pity. "How was your Christmas?"

"Lovely," Betty said. "We went to my daughter's, and everyone was there. We had a wonderful turkey dinner with all the fixings, played with our grandkids, and were home before dark—to a quiet, clean house. I never thought I'd say this, but it's nice to have passed the baton to the next generation." She pulled herself back. "I'm sorry. I shouldn't have... that was thoughtless."

"No... you have nothing to be sorry about. I'm glad to hear about your family. What kind of friend would I be if I couldn't be happy for you?"

Betty put her arm around Maisie's shoulders. "You are the best and bravest person I know."

"And—at the moment—the laziest. I haven't lifted a finger since I got here."

"Nonsense." Betty looked around the bakery. "I think we're ahead of schedule on everything. It'll be slow until New Year's Eve. We don't need any help here."

"You're sure?"

"Positive."

"Then I have something I want to talk to Josef about. Do you mind if I pop over to the diner? I'd like to catch him before he opens."

"You've got twenty minutes—you'd better get over there."

Maisie patted Betty's arm. "I'll be back in a jiffy." She pulled her coat off the hook by the door and traveled the short distance across the parking lot that separated the bakery building from the main diner. The neon Johanson's Diner sign glowed in the predawn darkness. The inside was brightly lit, and she could make out the familiar form of her husband of more than forty years as he raced from one end of the kitchen to the other. She suspected he'd love her idea. And she knew the feel of his arms around her would soothe her sad heart.

* * *

MAISIE OPENED the back door to the diner, and a rush of frigid air announced her arrival.

Josef's face broke into the smile that always settled on him when he saw her. "How's my best girl?"

Maisie's shoulders straightened as she walked into his outstretched arms. That man always knew how to lighten her spirits.

Josef rested his chin on top of her head and held her close.

He finally leaned to the side and whispered in her ear, "Feeling a bit blue?"

Maisie nodded her head against his shoulder.

"I know leaving the bakery isn't what you want to do, but it's for the best."

"I know. In my head, I know that. My heart hasn't caught up."

"It will. And I believe this will be the start of something better for you," he said, keeping his voice low.

She pulled back and looked into his eyes. "You really do, don't you?"

Josef nodded. "When God closes a door, he opens a window."

A smile played at the corner of Maisie's lips.

"How about a cup of coffee? It's just finished brewing."

"Half a cup," Maisie said. "That's all I'm allowed."

Josef moved to the coffee station and poured her a cup.

"I've never known you to drink a full cup, anyway."

Maisie chuckled. "That's true. I guess my doctor's restriction doesn't really affect me much."

Josef poured himself a cup, and they walked into the dining room, toward the front booth where they often shared coffee before Josef turned the sign to "Open."

"I've been thinking about our talk with Clara yesterday," Maisie said.

"Me, too," Josef said. "Her taking over the bakery is the answer to all our problems."

"I agree. Supplying the diner will help her and us, but she'd make a go of her patisserie without our business," Maisie said. "We couldn't keep her Christmas cookies in stock over here. People will be lined up around the block when she opens."

"It'll take months before she can get her new kitchen built

out and her permits in place. I hope people don't forget about her cookies."

Maisie raised a finger. "That's what I want to talk to you about. I think we can help her with that."

"Sure. We're going to put on our menu that all of our baked goods now come from Sweets & Treats."

"That'll help, for sure. I was also thinking that we could let her set up a bakery case in here." Maisie pointed to an open area next to the hostess stand. "There's room for one right there. She can showcase whatever she wants—to keep her name in the public eye."

"We can handle the sales for her here. Collect and submit the taxes for her. It'll draw people into the diner, too." Josef smiled.

"So, you like the idea?"

"I love the idea. I may even have a case we can clean up and let her use. I think we have one in the storage room off the back of the bakery."

"You know, I'm almost positive there's one in there."

They looked into each other's eyes and grinned conspiratorially.

"I can't wait to ask her about it," Maisie said.

Josef separated the slats of the window blinds and looked toward the motel parking lot. "I can see her car. She hasn't gone out yet."

"If I know her, she probably stayed up half the night making lists."

"I'll bet you're right. She'll stop here for breakfast when she gets up. Why don't we talk to her about it then?"

The lines of worry on Maisie's forehead disappeared in happy anticipation. She took a last sip of her coffee and stood. "It's time for you to open up. I'm going back to the bakery to have a look at that case. Call me when she comes over, okay?"

"Of course. I'll let you tell her about your great idea. I know it'll make her happy."

Maisie leaned in and kissed Josef's cheek before heading back to the bakery, this time with a spring in her step.

CHAPTER 4

Clara rolled over in bed, her foot sending her laptop to the edge where it teetered precariously before sliding onto the carpeted floor with a thunk. She sat bolt upright and scrambled to the floor. Clara opened the laptop and let out a whoosh of breath when the screen illuminated and displayed her login prompt.

The time showed it was six twenty-three. The sun wouldn't be up for over an hour. She had plenty of time to crawl back in bed for more much-needed sleep, but her mind started churning where she'd left off last night. She had so much to do before she could open her shop, and now that she had Noelle, she couldn't continue to stay at the motel while she leisurely looked for a new place to live.

Clara got to her feet and checked on Noelle. The dog was nestled into the blanket, snoring faintly. Clara headed for the shower. She'd pull herself together, complete the inventory spreadsheet she'd been working on when she'd fallen asleep, dig out her vision board of her dream bakery from the back of her SUV, and call her attorney.

This last item caused a fissure of fear to run through her. He'd given her his cell phone number so she could talk to him as soon as possible. Part of her wanted to call right then, but rousing him at this early hour wouldn't be appropriate. She'd waited this long—a little more wouldn't matter.

Clara showered and dressed, then took Noelle out and returned to the room to feed her. She completed her spreadsheet, saving the file. "This list will undoubtedly change before we open the patisserie," she told her dog, "but it contains enough detail to submit to the bank for a working capital loan."

Clara checked the time. It was now eight forty-eight. Surely that was a respectable hour to return a phone call from her attorney. She took a deep, steadying breath before placing the call.

Tom answered on the second ring. "Clara. Did you have a nice Christmas?"

"Yes. Fine. Thanks… You?"

"We did. My brother and his wife and kids are staying with us. We had a full house. It was very nice."

"Great," Clara said, willing Tom to get to the point of the call.

"I've got good news," he said.

Clara released the breath she'd been holding.

"The judge denied Travis's attempts to question your mental competency."

"I'm relieved to hear that," Clara said, "but I would have thought it would be obvious that I'm competent. My recent employment history should have been enough to substantiate that."

"We were able to use that to our advantage," Tom said, "but the fact that you took off without a backward glance and aren't making a claim on any of the marital assets gave the judge pause."

"What?"

"Not many people just walk away—especially from their share of a decently sized marital estate. With Travis being a dentist and you being a dietician at the hospital, the judge concluded that you'd have sizable assets."

"So, I'm nuts if I don't want any of it? When all I want is to get out of the marriage?"

"The judge needs to make sure that equity is done for both parties. He wants to make sure that you're not making a hasty decision."

"Whether I am or not, it's my decision." Clara's voice increased with her irritation.

Tom remained silent.

"Well—whatever. The judge denied Travis's motion or whatever it was. When do we get the final, signed papers? I'm anxious to get this divorce done."

"I'm afraid we have one more hoop to jump through," Tom said.

"Now what?" Clara attempted to keep her voice steady.

"Travis and his attorney put on quite a show at the hearing," Tom said. "About how stunned he was that you left—he had no clue anything was wrong—that maybe he'd neglected you by working such long hours…"

"By staying out with his girlfriend," Clara interrupted.

"We haven't put forth any proof of that."

"It's true! Are you doubting me?"

Noelle lifted her head off her paws and stared at Clara, who was now stomping from one end of the bed to the other.

"No. I'm sure he was. I'm just telling you we'd have to support that if we make the allegation in court. Anyway—I don't think we'll need to. The judge asked if the two of you had been to marriage counseling."

"We haven't."

"That's what Travis said. This judge likes to see that couples attempt to resolve their differences."

"It won't change anything. It'll just be a waste of time."

"Maybe so, but the judge made it a condition of his ruling against the competency inquiry."

"You've. Got. To. Be. Kidding."

"Look—before you say 'no'—think of it this way. It's fast and easy. We agreed to three sessions with a counselor on the court's approved list. The two of you will split the cost. It's not very expensive."

"Three? How long will that delay things?"

"We agreed to one a month."

Clara groaned. "That means we won't be divorced until March—or later."

"Competency hearings would have taken far longer. Worst case—your divorce will be final six to nine months after filing. All things considered, that's fast."

"Okay… okay. I'm sorry if I'm overreacting. I've decided to open a patisserie here and I've got my hands full setting up the business."

"Be careful with that," Tom advised. "You may want to wait until after your divorce. You don't want Travis to claim an interest in this new venture of yours."

"Seriously?" Clara's voice was shrill. "How in the world could he have an interest in it? It's all my effort and I'm using money I inherited."

"Don't get upset. Make sure you document every cent you spend and where it came from. That's all I'm saying. If you have any questions, ask me. Or have your business attorney call me."

Clara forced herself to breathe normally. "Where are these counselors located?"

"They are throughout the state," Tom said. "I know that you're not living here anymore. Do you have a preference where you go?"

"How about one along the western state line? That would be about a two-hour drive for each of us."

"Travis is going to claim he's too busy to take off work…"

"I don't care what Travis is going to claim! I'm busy, too, Tom. Starting a business is a lot of work. I shouldn't have to drive all the way back there for these stupid counseling sessions."

"All right. I'll make it happen."

"I'd appreciate that."

"I'm sorry this isn't moving along as quickly as you'd like," Tom said. "These things never do. We will get your divorce finalized."

"I know. One more thing?"

"Yes."

"Don't tell Travis or his attorney that I'm opening a patisserie. It's none of their business. I don't want Travis to know."

"Of course not. But he may find out, eventually. It'll be a matter of public record."

Clara sucked air in through her teeth. "I know."

"I'll be in touch next week about the counseling."

"I don't care who the counselor is. I just want it to be as soon and as convenient as possible."

"Understood. Happy New Year, Clara."

"Thank you, Tom. The same to you."

Clara punched off the call and slapped her palm against

the wall. As if she wasn't already busy enough, she'd have to devote more time to Travis.

Noelle stood and came to her mistress, putting her paws on Clara's leg and wagging her tail.

"It's okay, girl. It's just one more hurdle to clear." Clara dropped to her knees and nuzzled her furry companion. "We'll get through it. Travis isn't going to stop us."

Clara stood. "You stay right here," she commanded as she shoved her arms through the sleeves of her down jacket. "Let me get my vision board out of the car to show you. I've got pictures of the baked goods we'll offer and the space for tables and chairs. I've even got paint chips for the wall colors. We're going to have the most fashionable patisserie outside of Paris. Just wait until you see what I've got planned!"

CHAPTER 5

Clara entered the diner mid-morning. "I have a takeout order," she said to Mary as the young server straightened menus at the hostess stand. The dining room was vacant except for a young couple in the far corner.

Clara looked around. She'd never seen the diner so deserted. As Josef said, everyone must be at the mall, scarfing up after-Christmas bargains.

Mary grabbed a menu from the top of the stack and started toward a booth along the wall.

"I won't need that," Clara said, calling her back. "I'm not dining in."

Mary turned back to her. "Josef said to seat you here when you came in."

"I can't stay," Clara said. "I've got my dog in the car."

"Since when did you get a dog?" Mary asked. She looked at Clara and chuckled. "You adopted one of the strays that Josef is always rescuing, didn't you?"

"How'd you know?"

"I have two of them myself."

"Noelle's in the car. It's too cold to leave her out there—and the motel doesn't allow pets—so I figure she'll have to go everywhere with me until I find a new place to live."

"Now it makes sense," Mary said. "Josef said to seat you and your little friend in the booth. He must have been talking about your dog."

Both women laughed.

"Go get—what's her name—Noelle, while I tell Josef you're here. I'll find your order and bring it to your table."

The young couple approached Mary, paid their check, and headed out into the morning.

"Okay," Clara said. "I guess there's nobody in here to notice a dog."

Clara brought Noelle into the diner on her leash, admonishing her to be on her best behavior. She was no sooner seated, with Noelle curled up under her feet, and her order of steel-cut oatmeal in front of her, when Josef and Maisie joined her. Josef carried a dish of crispy bacon with him.

"Good morning, dear," Maisie said. "Did you sleep well?"

"Honestly, no. If I got more than three or four hours, I'd be surprised. My mind kept working through all the things I need to do. Not the least of which is to find a new place to live before the motel tosses me out for having a pet."

"Don't worry too much about that. I've known the owner for years. His bark is worse than his bite. He won't kick you out," Josef said, slipping a piece of bacon to Noelle under the table.

"Good to know, but I need to find myself a permanent place to live, now that I'm calling Pinewood home." Clara spooned brown sugar over her oatmeal and topped it with fresh blueberries. "How about the two of you?" She looked directly at Maisie. "How was the rest of your evening?"

"Fine," Maisie said. "But I tossed and turned all night, too."

"Are you having second thoughts?" Clara's head came up. "About me opening a competing bakery?"

"Not at all," Josef assured her.

"We've been thinking about things that will help make you successful."

"Buying from me is more than enough. And allowing me to use your bakery until I'm up and running. Not to mention allowing me to poach your staff."

Josef waved a hand in dismissal. "That's nothing."

"We've had another idea," Maisie said, her eyes shining. "We thought we'd let you keep a case here that would stock your baked goods."

Clara's hand halted, her spoon halfway to her mouth. "What a genius idea. That'll keep my name in front of everyone. It'll also allow me to test items to see what people really want. Filled croissants or plain? Scones or muffins? Artisan breads or more traditional offerings? That will let me refine my menu without a lot of expensive trial and error. Gosh…" She brought her hand to her heart.

"That's exactly what we thought." Maisie's voice resonated with pleasure.

"Where can I get a case?" She looked at Josef. "I'm going to need them for the patisserie, too."

"I know where to send you," he said. "But we have a case in storage that you can use in the diner. It just needs to be cleaned and polished."

"When can I start on it?"

"I'll take care of all that," Josef said.

"No way! I can't allow that. You're doing so much for me already."

"I want to do this," he said. "I'll have time today or tomorrow."

"You were right about it being dead in here today," Clara said, looking around the dining room.

"It'll be like this until New Year's Eve."

"Speaking of which, do you have a special dessert planned?"

He shook his head.

"Why don't I supply one? We can use it to kick off the introduction of my bakery."

"That's smart marketing," Maisie said. "Are you sure you'll have time?"

"Positive. Plus, I'll enjoy it. I've been away from the bakery for two mornings and I miss it already."

"Do you have something in mind?"

"I've been going through my recipes, deciding which ones I should offer in the patisserie. I came up with a cranberry lime cheesecake that I think would be perfect on New Year's Eve. Decadent and seasonal with the cranberries, but lime cuts down on the sweetness and lightens it up. It's very pretty, too."

"I can't wait to try it," Josef said, slipping another piece of bacon to the open mouth under the table.

"Then we've got a plan. How many slices do you think you'll need?"

"I'll bet we'll need at least a hundred—and I'm sure we could sell two hundred. If you have a photo, I'll post it, and we can take orders for full cheesecakes, too."

"I'll plan on making fourteen full cheesecakes, plus the special orders." Clara flushed with a surge of excitement. She was about to make the first item for her new business. "I'll get you the list of ingredients I'll need," she said to Maisie.

"This will be our first collaboration," Maisie said. "I'll style the case with silver glitter, so it looks very festive." Her toe tapped with excitement. "And to think, this time yesterday, I was so down in the dumps—thinking I was about to lose my contact with the baking world."

"Just goes to show how different things can look in a day." Josef stuck out his hand to Clara. "To our new relationship."

Clara took his hand and shook it, followed by Maisie's. "I cannot tell you how much I appreciate your enthusiasm and your help." Her voice grew ragged. "It means the world to me."

Noelle put her muzzle on Josef's lap and nudged his leg. He gave another strip of bacon.

"Don't forget that my consulting services come with the purchase of the bakery equipment," Josef said. "I'm here to help in any way I can."

"Thank you, Josef. I'll take you up on that."

"I mean it. Don't you forget."

"I won't," Clara assured him.

Noelle uttered a hoarse "woof" and Josef handed her the last strip of bacon.

CHAPTER 6

Clara turned into the alley that ran behind the row of shops in the downtown area, hoping to find dedicated parking behind the space she planned to rent. She drove toward the end of the block and was happy to spot Kurt's vehicle tucked into a spot behind the building. She nestled her SUV next to his.

Noelle hopped off the back seat and rested her front paws on the console.

"You're coming in with me," Clara said. "And, again, you need to be on your best behavior. Kurt won't have bacon to feed you." She stroked Noelle on the top of her head. "I'm not going to give you people food—it's not good for you—so don't get used to it."

Noelle wagged her tail as Clara got out of the car and opened the rear door, grabbing the leash. Noelle paused.

"Come on," Clara commanded.

Noelle poked her nose at the vision board that was resting on the floor. She continued to wag her tail.

"Do you think I should take that in with me?"

Noelle gave a short "Woof."

Clara laughed and picked up the board, tucking it under her arm. "If you insist. Now, come on!"

Noelle sprang to the pitted asphalt.

Clara approached the gray, utilitarian metal door with the street number and word ENTRANCE painted in black, but stopped and reversed course before they reached it. Instead, they made their way around the building toward the front door. "I want to enter my patisserie for the very first time through the front door," Clara said. "I want to feel what it will be like to step in, off the street. Does that make sense?"

Noelle looked up at her mistress and wagged her tail faster.

They walked by the large, plate-glass window. The afternoon sun glinted off it, producing a mirrored effect. Clara made a mental note to have the glass treated with anti-reflective film. She'd want people driving by on the street to be able to see the baked goods in the window displays she'd have.

She cupped her hand to the window and pressed her face to the glass. The overhead lights were switched on. The interior was bright and cheerful. She was struck, once again, by how perfect the black-and-white checkered flooring was for a patisserie. It was exactly what she'd pinned to the vision board under her arm. Kurt had told her he had operated his law practice from the space until he'd joined a larger firm and moved into their offices. She'd love to ask him why he'd had such unlawyerly decor, but thought that line of inquiry might be rude. It was, she realized, none of her business.

The front door stood slightly ajar. Kurt was nowhere to be seen.

Clara pushed the door open, calling, "Hello! Kurt?" as she and Noelle made their way inside.

Kurt appeared in an open doorway at the back of the space. "Hi, you two." He dropped to one knee and Clara unhooked the leash.

Noelle raced to Kurt and licked his face while he gave her a vigorous rubdown.

"I wanted to get all the lights on and the heat turned up before you got here."

"We're early—I'm sorry. I couldn't wait any longer."

Kurt rose, smiling at her. "I figured you would be. You're going to make your dreams come true here—if you still think the space meets your needs after you take a good look at it."

Clara spun around slowly. Swaths of sunshine traversed the room.

Noelle circled three times, then settled herself in the warmth of a sunny spot. She rolled on her side and closed her eyes.

"I think someone needs a nap," Kurt said.

Clara stifled a yawn. "I think we both do. I was so excited last night, I could barely sleep." She stretched and walked to the window. "I think there's plenty of room here to build a four-foot by eight-foot platform." She paced out the footprint. "I'd like to create window displays with tiered glass shelving."

"That would be very eye-catching. The other shopkeepers along here tell me that their window displays draw in customers."

She turned around and took giant steps to the back of the space, counting as she went. "I'll put a row of baskets along the rear wall for breads and baguettes. There's enough room along here for three or four display cases for croissants, cakes, cookies, and pies," she motioned with one hand, keeping the vision board clamped to her side with the other arm.

"My mouth is watering, just thinking about it," he said.

"That leaves plenty of space for five or six tables with chairs between the cases and the window." She gestured to the side wall. "I'll put a coffee station over there."

"You've thought this through, haven't you?"

Clara cut her eyes to his. "I've been planning this patisserie since I was in high school." She paused, then pushed on. "Would you like to see my vision board? Promise you won't tease me?"

"I'd find it very helpful," he said, his tone serious. "The lease will include a tenant improvement budget, so—as your landlord—I need to know what you want. As for teasing you? I'd never do that. I admire anyone who has a dream and the courage to bring it to life."

Clara felt herself flush and cleared her throat. She took the board from under her arm and held it out in front of her.

Kurt stepped to her side.

The board was covered with photos clipped from magazines, paint chips, fabric samples, recipes, lists, and more lists.

Kurt bent and examined each item with care. When he finished, he whistled softly. "You've covered everything. I've helped hundreds of people set up new businesses and the vast majority of them encounter costly delays because of indecision and lack of preparation." His eyes telegraphed admiration. "That's not going to be a problem for you."

Clara blushed again. "Thank you. I hope so. I've obviously never done this before, so I'm not sure I know what I'm doing."

"No one is completely prepared—there were things I didn't account for when I opened my law practice—but you learn and adjust as you go."

"Really? Like what?"

Kurt chuckled. "When you open a law practice in a

building with a historic designation—like this one—you won't be able to change the original black-and-white checkered flooring."

Clara laughed. "I wondered about that. It's perfect for a patisserie, but... What did you do?"

"I spent a fortune on oriental rugs and covered it up."

"It's in beautiful shape," Clara said, bending at the waist to inspect the flooring. "I guess I'm the beneficiary of that." She removed a paint chip from her vision board and laid it against the floor. She straightened and walked around the paint chip in a five-foot radius. "I like it. No, I love it! What do you think?"

"A soft, sunny yellow will be a nice change from the stodgy taupe color that I chose for my firm." He stooped and picked up the chip. "Whipped butter," he read. "What an apt name."

"Right?"

He handed her back the chip. "Your tenant improvements will include painting. We can get started on this right away."

"Can I see the rest of the space?"

"Of course. The restrooms are over there." He pointed to an alcove containing two marked doors. "The fixtures were updated three years ago, so they should be fine."

"I'd like to change the signs from Men and Women to Monsieur and Madame."

"Easy enough. And here," he led her to the room he had been in when she'd arrived, "is my former file room. If we knock out this wall," he pointed, "and open the space up to the conference room on the other side, I think you'll have ample room for your kitchen."

"Combined, this should be plenty of room. I'll need three sinks—one for hand washing, one for food preparation, and one for dish washing. The bread ovens will be gas and I'll require 220-volt electricity for the steam oven."

"Running those lines will be the most time-consuming part of the process. I've got a detailed floor plan of the space back at my office that I can give you."

Clara closed her eyes and hugged herself. This was going to happen. She would have her patisserie. "I've seen enough."

"You're ready to sign a lease? I don't want to rush you. Maybe take a day or two to think about it? At least look at other possibilities—"

Clara shook her head as he spoke. "Nope. This is it." She tapped her vision board with her index finger. "You can see it for yourself. I've been creating this exact space in my mind and heart for years."

"Okay, then. Let's wake up that snoring dog of yours and head to my office."

CHAPTER 7

Clara took the elevator to the top floor of the tallest building in Pinewood. Hodson, Williams, and Holbrook occupied half of the fourth floor. The thick rug muffled her footsteps in the lobby. She wondered if it was one that Kurt had brought with him from the store front she was about to lease. She felt underdressed in jeans, lug-soled boots, a sweater, and her long down jacket. With Noelle at her side, she must look completely out of place.

The woman looked at her over the top of the heavy mahogany reception station and pushed an infinitesimal strand of gray hair back into place behind her ears. She ran her eyes over Clara and Noelle, and it was clear she didn't approve.

"I'm here to see Kurt," Clara said. "I have an appointment."

"Let me check Mr. Holbrook's calendar," the woman said with overt formality. "Ahhh... Clara Conway?"

"That's right."

"Why don't you take a seat," she gestured to a leather

Chesterfield sofa set against a wall. "I'll let him know that you —and your *dog*—are here to see him." Her tone was stiff.

"He knows Noelle will be with me," Clara said as she and Noelle went to the sofa. She'd no sooner settled herself and picked up a copy of the morning newspaper from an end table when Kurt came around a corner and into the lobby.

"Come on back," he said. "Do we have anything we can use as a dog's water bowl?" he asked the receptionist.

The woman's lips settled into a hard line. "I'm sure I don't know."

"Just go into the kitchen and find something, okay? Then bring it to my office," he said, ignoring the woman's prickliness. "Would you like a cup of coffee?" he asked Clara as they made their way to his office.

"That'd be great," she said. "I think my lack of sleep is catching up to me."

"I've got a single cup brewer in my office," he replied. "I drink far too much coffee. It's my one vice." He opened the door to a corner office with a sweeping view past the downtown to the state university campus on the horizon. The landscape was peppered with trees, now barren in winter. The late afternoon sunshine washed the scene in a brittle brightness.

Clara stepped to the windows. "What a beautiful town. I'll bet this is a gorgeous view when the leaves are on the trees."

"It is. And you should see it in fall. You'll have to come back, just for the view."

"I may hold you to that," Clara said. "Pinewood is a charming town."

"And as soon as you sign this lease, it'll be your hometown." He motioned her to a round conference table in the corner where papers were arranged in neat rows. He inserted a pod into the coffee machine and pressed the brew button. "Cream or sugar?" he asked as the machine whirred.

"Black's fine," she said.

The receptionist knocked on the partially open door, then pushed in and set a soup bowl of water on the floor.

Noelle tugged to get to it, and Clara dropped the leash. "Thank you," she called to the woman as she returned to the reception desk.

Noelle noisily lapped up a drink, then returned to Clara's side.

Kurt set cups of coffee in front of each of them and worked his way through the paperwork spread out on the table.

They agreed on the lease and the details of the tenant improvements Kurt would provide in short order. The recitation of the necessary licenses and permits was exactly what Clara had expected. The discussion of her new business entity —the limited liability company—was the only sticking point.

"So, I can form a single-member limited liability company and it will accomplish my taxation objectives, but it may not shield me from liability in the way that a regular limited liability company would?"

"That's correct. If you elect to go with a single member LLC, your liability insurance will probably be much more expensive."

"Gosh—I hadn't expected this."

"What about adding someone else as a member? You wouldn't have to give up control or share much of the profit. Your operating agreement for the limited liability company could handle those issues. Do you know anyone you could ask to go in with you on the patisserie, even in a tiny way? A family member or friend?"

Clara pursed her lips, putting her elbows on the table and resting her head in her hands. "My mother was my only family, and she… she died recently."

"What about friends?"

Clara shook her head. "Everyone's back in Glenn Hills. I left there because I wanted to leave it all behind me. I can't see asking anyone there to join me in a business venture here."

Kurt remained silent, rolling his pen between his fingers.

Clara cocked her head to one shoulder and looked at him. "What do you think about Josef? He—and Maisie—have been so enthusiastic about my patisserie and have been so generous in their offers of help. You know him better than I do. Should I ask him if he wants to be a member of Sweets & Treats, LLC?"

Kurt stared back at her, a smile spreading across his face. "That's exactly who you should ask. I think he'd be delighted."

"We haven't known each other long and I would hate for him to think I'm trying to take advantage of him."

"He wouldn't need to contribute financially. He could provide expertise and advice."

"I could use both!"

"I can prepare an operating agreement that will be fair to both of you. It's a terrific solution." He leaned back in his chair. "As I said, we need to get your LLC formed before you sign your lease and apply for permits. It's really the first step."

"I'll talk to Josef in the morning. Do you think he'll need you to explain this to him?"

"Josef is a very business-savvy guy. He's on several boards around town. He'll understand what you're asking him. Why don't you talk to him? Then both of you can come in together and we can discuss the structure of your business relationship. I'll be the attorney for the LLC. That means you each should have another attorney review the paperwork from your individual perspectives."

"Oh boy," Clara said, twisting her hands. "This is getting complicated. I don't know any other business lawyers."

"I can recommend several. I know it seems like a lot, but you want to start things on a good footing."

"You're right. I do. I've been so wrapped up in recipes and decor that I didn't think about all of this boring business stuff." She bit her lip. "Sorry. I know this is what you do for a living. I didn't mean to offend you."

"You haven't. I love what I do, but it's not everyone's bag. I think we've done everything we can for now. It's getting late," he said, turning to his view where the sun was slipping below the horizon. "If you don't have dinner plans, why don't I introduce you to the best pizza place in town? It's early. I think we can sneak Noelle in the back with us."

"That would be wonderful," Clara said. "I haven't eaten since mid-morning, and I'm starved."

Clara woke the sleepy canine, and they made their way through the lobby.

"I'm calling it quits a bit early tonight," Kurt said to the receptionist.

The woman looked up. "I just finished typing a message that came in for you. You must not have seen it."

"Can it wait until morning?"

She shook her head.

"Give me a second," Kurt said to Clara. "I'll be right back." He retraced his steps to his office.

Clara and Noelle returned to the sofa along the wall. An incoming call drew the receptionist's attention and Clara and Noelle waited.

Kurt joined them after another ten minutes, but this time

he didn't have his coat with him. "I'm afraid you're going to have to give me a rain check," he said.

Clara stood. "Of course. I hope nothing's wrong?" His face was drawn, and sadness hung heavy on him.

"One of my best clients and oldest friends has died. I've known him my entire life. His son—his only child—is traveling in a remote area of China and can't get home for another week. I'm an executor of the estate. I just spoke briefly to his son, and he's asked me to step in to make funeral arrangements and begin necessary paperwork until he can return."

"I'm so sorry. I can see that this is upsetting for you."

Kurt shrugged.

"You go do what you need to do. If I can help in any way—if you need to talk—you know how to find me."

"I'm sorry about dinner."

"Don't give it another thought."

"Let me know when you've spoken to Josef. We need to move your paperwork for the LLC along as quickly as possible. I'll send you the names of a couple of other attorneys for you to consider—to represent your interests."

"That's the least of your considerations right now, but thank you."

"I'll talk to you in the next couple of days," Kurt said. "Thank you for understanding."

"Be kind to yourself," Clara said as she and Noelle headed for the door.

CHAPTER 8

Clara rolled over in bed and opened one eye. Her laptop lay next to her, the screen open but dark. The battery must have run down during the night. The last time she'd checked the time, it was after two.

Noelle whined and scratched at the door with her paw. Bright sunshine played at the edges of the motel blackout curtains. Clara picked up her phone. It was almost ten.

"Sorry, girl," Clara said, throwing off the covers and scrambling to her feet.

Noelle whimpered urgently.

Clara stuck her feet into her thick slippers and threw on her down jacket over her pajama top. Noelle had to go out—now. Clara never should have slept so late. She fervently hoped no one would see her, with her bed head and outlandish attire. She'd take Noelle to the grassy area outside their door, then hurry back into her room.

Clara clipped the leash on the animal who was now leaping frantically against the door and stepped out into the bright morning. Noelle tugged her along until they reached their destination.

Clara shielded her eyes from the sun with one hand while she waited for Noelle to finish. "Good girl," she said, swiveling to retreat to their room and bumping into the front desk manager.

"Oh," she said, stepping back. "I'm sorry. I didn't hear you come up."

"Miss Conway, is it?"

Clara nodded, pulling her jacket close and wishing she'd taken the time to zip it. She must look like a lunatic.

"I see you've got a dog with you."

Clara swallowed hard. There was no denying it.

"As you know, we don't allow pets at the Pinewood Springs Motel."

"I know." Clara averted her eyes. "I'm sorry. I just got her… I haven't had her the whole time I've been here. I was only going to be here for a short time, but then my car repair got delayed again and again." She knew she was rambling like an idiot. "And then I offered to take this stray that Josef had found to the shelter on Christmas Eve, but they were closed—so what was I to do? I had to bring her here. And now I've decided to stay. In Pinewood."

The man held up a hand to stop her. "I just talked to Josef. I understand your predicament. He told me you'll be moving into a permanent residence soon. That's why I came down here." He held up a sheaf of papers. "I wanted to bring you the local newsprint insert that advertises homes for sale and apartments for rent, together with a detailed map of Pinewood. I thought they might be helpful."

Clara looked at him and noticed, for the first time, that his eyes were kind and expression soft. "That's… that's so nice of you." She continued to stare at him. "So, you're not kicking me out—for having Noelle?"

The man shook his head. "Of course not. She's not doing any harm."

"How do you know that?"

"Housekeeping told me she's house trained and hasn't chewed anything."

"How did they know I had a dog? I hid her food and toys every morning before we left for the day. She's never been left alone in my room. And she doesn't bark."

"Are you kidding? Housekeepers always know."

"So, when did you find out?"

"From the very beginning. I didn't think Christmas was the time to approach you about your dog."

"I'll be finding a new place to live as soon as possible," Clara said.

"That'll be great," the man said. "I can't ignore her forever, but you can keep Noelle here with you until you find a place. You've been a pleasure to have as a guest."

Clara beamed at him. "Thank you." If everyone in Pinewood was this nice, she would love living here.

* * *

FORTY MINUTES LATER, a freshly showered Clara pushed through the door of the diner with Noelle at her side. She saw Josef in the pass through to the kitchen where orders were placed for servers to pick up. Breakfast was over and the lunch rush hadn't started yet. There were no plates waiting under warmers. She raised her hand and caught his attention.

"Clara! I thought we might not see you this morning."

"I've been staying up way too late—I can't seem to turn my

brain off—and then I'm sleeping in. I need to get my body clock back onto baker's time."

Josef chuckled. "There'll be time for all of that. Are you here to eat?" He bent to pat Noelle. "I can get some bacon ready in a jiffy."

"I'm here to see you, actually. And no more bacon for this one," she admonished. "Bacon's not good for her."

"I know. Sorry, girl." He directed the comment to Noelle. "So—what can I help you with?"

"Let's step into your office. I know the lunch rush is about to start, so I'll be brief."

"Sure. As a matter of fact, I've gotten out all my files on the business permits that you'll need. I've made you copies of every application you'll need to fill out. I've also got sample forms of financial statements that you can use when applying to vendors for credit—after you get your bank account established."

They stepped into his office, and he pointed to the neat stack of papers on one corner of his desk. "You'll need this as soon as you get your LLC set up."

"Thank you for all of this, Josef." She gestured to the papers. "I'm feeling overwhelmed by everything I have to do, to be honest with you."

"There's a lot to setting yourself up in business," he replied. "Just take it a step at a time. It'll all come together, and there's no need to rush. I'm always here to help you—anything you need."

He sat in one of the two chairs in front of his desk and waved her into the other chair. Noelle settled herself between them.

Clara unwound the scarf from her neck and licked her lips. "I'm so grateful to you for everything you—and Maisie—

have done for me."

"We were glad to do it. You know that."

Clara nodded. "I've come to ask you if you'd be willing to do something else. It's a big ask, so don't hesitate to say 'no.' " She forced herself to raise her eyes to his. "I'm not sure I even want to broach this subject. I don't want to offend you."

"Whatever it is, I'm certain you won't be doing that." He rested his elbows on his knees and reached out one hand to pat her arm. "Just ask me."

"I was wondering—hoping—Kurt suggested I ask you: would you consider becoming a member of my LLC? He advised against doing business as a single-member LLC, so I'll need another member." She rocked back in her chair and watched him.

"I don't think I'd like to be a member," he said softly.

"No. Of course not. I'm sorry I asked. I was out of line." She began to stand.

"I think Maisie should be your other member." Josef grinned. "She's the baker in the family and this would give her something new to focus on."

Clara lowered herself back into the chair.

"Giving up the bakery has been hard for Maisie, emotionally. She's still rehabbing from her stroke, and she's been depressed and dispirited. This will give her a much-needed shot in the arm."

"That's a genius suggestion. I'd love that!" Clara clasped her hands to her chest. "I won't take advantage of her. I promise. I'll do all the work. She will just be there as a consultant—a sounding board."

"I know that you'd never do anything to harm Maisie. If I thought otherwise, I wouldn't have suggested this."

"Do you think she'll be interested?"

"I know she will be. She's said over and over that she wishes she were younger so she could work at your patisserie." Josef shifted back in his chair. "I hoped that—once you got up and running—there might be a part-time job for her there. After all these years running a bakery operation, she'll be bored sitting at home."

"You can count on it. I'd be so lucky to have her. Everyone in town knows and loves Maisie. She'll attract customers."

Josef nodded his agreement.

"Is Maisie here? Should I talk to her now?"

"She's at her physical therapy session. They exhaust her, so she'll go home for a nap. What are you doing later today?"

"I just talked to the front-desk manager." Clara gave Josef a rueful smile. "I guess you already know what I'm going to say. He said he talked to you."

"He's a very nice guy. They won't kick you out because of Noelle."

"That's what he said. I still need to find a place to live, so I'm apartment hunting this afternoon."

"There are a lot of rentals by the university and many of them allow dogs," Josef said.

"That's what I'm hoping. I'll want to rent for a year, then buy my own place. It's just too much to think about househunting right now."

"That's smart. You should get to know Pinewood better, so you know where you'd like to live."

"I was going to give Kurt a call, too—to let him know about the LLC."

"I'm sure Maisie will jump at the chance. Why don't I call Kurt and discuss it with him? He can start the paperwork. We'll both need to have our separate attorneys review it."

"Kurt said that, too. He also told me you're extremely business savvy."

The color rose in Josef's cheeks, and she could tell her remark pleased him.

"I'll reach out to him now. Why don't you come by the house tonight to talk to Maisie?"

"Perfect. Maybe seven?"

"Make it five. We can talk over dinner."

Clara opened her mouth to protest.

"We have to eat," Josef said. "One more person is nothing. I'll bring home something from the diner. Now—off you go." He stood. "We've both got a lot to do today."

CHAPTER 9

Clara drove past the impressive brick arch that marked the main entrance to the campus. School was on winter break and there were only a handful of people walking along the pathways weaving between old gothic buildings that were part of the original university. In the distance, she could make out unadorned block and glass structures that would evidence more recent and budget-conscious additions to the facilities. "We'll come here another time to explore," she said to Noelle. "I love a college campus, don't you?"

Noelle thumped her tail against the back seat in response.

"Right now, we don't have time. I've circled six places I think we should look at." She glanced into the back seat. "They all allow dogs. Don't worry."

Clara's GPS directed her to take a left in a quarter mile. She moved into the left lane, spotted Windsor Lane up ahead, and turned as directed. The street was narrow, with tall trees on either side, their roots causing the sidewalks to crack and buckle. Two-story, narrow apartment buildings occupied both sides of the street. Cars lined each curb, leaving a narrow lane in the center of the street for her to traverse. One or two of the buildings looked freshly painted and renovated, but most of them wore an air of benign neglect.

Clara's GPS announced she had arrived at her destination. She double-checked the street number on the building with the one on her list and her heart sank. She was in the right place.

She drove further up the block until she found an opening at the curb. She maneuvered her SUV into the small space, cursing under her breath at the difficulty of the task. "I've either got to polish up my parallel parking skills, or we'll need to get a compact car," she muttered to Noelle.

They got out of the car and made their way back to the apartment building that advertised they welcomed small dogs and had an immediate vacancy. Clara looked for an intercom or buzzer by the glass door into the small lobby and realized that there wasn't one. She pulled on the long metal handle and the door opened. Access wasn't secured—anyone could enter. Clara pursed her lips and moved down the long hall to number 11. A sign affixed to the door said "Manager."

Clara knocked and waited, taking in the peeling paint on the walls and the threadbare carpet

"Coming," came a woman's voice from behind the door.

Clara continued to wait. There was a peephole in the door, and she imagined that the woman on the other side was checking her out. Clara heard a series of deadbolts being unlocked before the door was opened on a chain.

"Yeah," said the woman, a cigarette hanging on her lower lip. A paroxysm of coughing erupted from her, and she grabbed for the cigarette.

"I'm here about the apartment," Clara said.

The woman looked her over carefully, then rested her eyes on Noelle. "We charge extra for her, ya know."

"I read that in your listing, yes."

"It's a two-bedroom on the second floor. The elevator's out, so you gotta take the stairs. You wanna see it?" The woman turned aside as another wave of coughing washed over her.

Clara took a step back.

Noelle began pulling at the leash, sniffing at something along the baseboard.

Clara turned her head to look and recoiled at what she saw. A cockroach skittered away, with Noelle in hot pursuit.

Would Clara—ever—in a million years want to live here?

"No!"

The force of her response caused the woman to recoil. "You don't have to yell," the woman replied before slamming the door in Clara's face.

"Leave it," Clara commanded as she pulled Noelle away from her prey. "We're outta here. The others have to be better than this."

They set out, again, in pursuit of a new home. Of the remaining candidates Clara had selected, three were worse and one looked to be about the same as the first apartment they'd visited. The only viable one had been rented that morning.

"We've struck out on all counts today," Clara told Noelle. "Time to come up with a new plan. What do you say we stop at that flower shop near our new patisserie to pick up flowers to take to Maisie and Josef? You're supposed to take a hostess gift when you go to someone's house for dinner, you know."

Noelle let out a short "woof."

Clara arrived at the florist shortly before four. She selected an enormous bunch of stargazer lilies and had the florist tie them with a bright blue ribbon.

"We've got forty-five minutes to kill before we head over to Maisie and Josef's for dinner. How about we take a walk down some of these residential streets? Our shop is close to here—this will be our neighborhood. Sort of, anyway."

Clara stowed the flowers in her car before they crossed the street and began their leisurely trek into the historic neighborhood next to the downtown shopping district.

Sidewalks were wide, and handsome two- and three-story brick homes sat at the back of generous sloping lawns. Every home had at least one tall, graceful tree in front.

"This will be so beautiful when the leaves come back," Clara said. "It's even pretty now."

Noelle wagged her tail as she pranced along.

They reached the end of the long block and crossed over to come back on the other side of the street. Clara was almost to the main street when a sign in the window of a well-tended Victorian caught her eye.

Furnished Guest House For Rent
Ideal for a Single Occupant

A phone number was listed.

Clara stopped and surveyed the facade. The brick exterior rose two full stories, with a small, square turret rising to a third. Large bay windows dominated both the first and second floors. A porch wrapped around the front and disappeared out of view. White lace curtains gleamed in every window. An evergreen wreath hung on the door.

Clara pulled Noelle to her, and they walked cautiously up the driveway. She wanted to catch a glimpse of the guest house.

They were almost even with the edge of the house when

her hopes were rewarded. A quaint brick cottage sat behind the main house, along the rear property line.

Clara's breath came fast. "It's like a mini version of the first floor of the main house," she whispered to Noelle. "It's even got a bay window!"

No lights emanated from the guest house, and it was shrouded in the shadow of the main house, but Clara had seen enough. She knew this would be the place for them. Clara whipped her phone out of her purse and punched in the number. She listened as the number rang, but no one answered. It didn't even click over to a voicemail.

Clara made sure that she'd dialed the correct number and that it was saved into her phone. If it wasn't too late when she got back to the motel tonight, she'd call back.

Clara and Noelle returned to her car. "I think we've found our new home," she said as Noelle hopped into place in the back seat. Clara was excited to see Maisie. What had started as a day with questions might end up as a day with answers.

CHAPTER 10

Clara rang the doorbell shortly before five, the enormous bouquet of lilies almost obscuring her face. Noelle stood quietly next to her.

Maisie opened the door and put on a smile that didn't match the rest of her appearance. Her shoulders sagged; her hair was out of place. The cardigan she wore was buttoned in the wrong holes and hung askew.

"These are for you," Clara stated the obvious. "They're just starting to open, so they should last all week."

"Thank you, dear," Maisie said as she moved aside and beckoned them to step inside. "They're lovely." She took the bouquet from Clara. "Let's get these into water."

Clara followed her, past the darkened living room, and into the kitchen. "Were you lying down when I got here?" She'd never seen Maisie looking disheveled.

"No. I was sitting in the living room. Thinking. I know it was getting dark in there, but I hadn't gotten around to turning on the lights." Maisie pointed to the cabinet above the refrigerator. "Can you open that for me? That's where I keep my best vases."

Clara's height allowed her to open the cabinet without using a step stool. "Which one?"

"My favorite is the tall cut glass on the right. It was a wedding present and I've always loved it."

Clara carefully lifted the heavy, lead glass vase to the counter and filled it with water.

Maisie began cutting each stem and passing the flowers to Clara to arrange in the vase.

"These are my favorite," Maisie said. "Thank you. I needed something to cheer me up. How did you know?"

"I'd like to claim to be prescient, but this was just dumb luck—or maybe divine intervention. What's going on?"

"I'm feeling rudderless—adrift. What should I be doing with this last chapter of my life? I still love to bake. Working with the ingredients—trying new combinations of flavors—is something I truly adore. And I enjoyed working with the other women. I can still bake things here," she swept her arm in an arc, "but there's only so much I can give to the neighbors. Before long, they'll be acting like they're not home when they see me coming up their walkways."

Clara laughed. "I doubt that, but I understand where you're coming from. These big life changes can be unsettling, even if you're the one initiating them."

"Exactly. Are you feeling… unsettled? You're certainly uprooting your life."

"Overwhelmed might be a better word for it. There's so much to do. I feel like everything in my life is changing."

"Except your love of baking."

"True."

"You're making these changes because you want to. I'm doing it because of my stroke. I never wanted that."

"We were both forced into a new life by things that we didn't want and couldn't control. For me, it was a cheating husband whose latest infidelity was the last straw."

"Oh, honey, I had no idea. I knew you were in the middle of a divorce, but I didn't know the circumstances." Maisie pulled out a chair at the kitchen table. "Josef should be home in half an hour. Will you put the flowers here and we'll sit and enjoy them? The kitchen is my favorite room in this house."

Clara placed the vase on the sturdy maple table. "I can see why," she said, considering the room. The wallpaper was a lattice-work design, adorned with strawberries and roses. Warm pine cabinets lined the exterior walls. A large window above the farmhouse sink was framed in starched white lace curtains. Looking like it had stepped out of the eighties, the room was spotlessly clean and enticingly worn. Anyone buying this house in today's market would tear this kitchen down to the studs, Clara thought, and that would be a shame. This room—reflecting Maisie's touch—was comforting and inviting beyond measure.

Clara sat opposite her friend. "I had been out of town, attending to my mother in the hospital, when she died unexpectedly. I stayed on to deal with her estate and came home a day early. I wanted to surprise Travis. Only I was the one who got the surprise. He'd been spending the night with his dental hygienist—he's a dentist—the whole time I'd been gone. He'd sworn that he'd broken it off with her. That, of course, was a lie. I couldn't take it anymore. While he was spending the night with *her*—I drove by her house on my way into town and found his car there—I packed up the few things from our life together that I wanted to keep and started driving."

"Wow. That took *chutzpah*."

"I guess. Anyway, I didn't want anything from him—I only wanted my freedom. I had inherited enough money from my mom to start my patisserie—the one I'd been planning for years—so I loaded my car and drove. I figured I'd know when I came to the right place to open my patisserie and restart my life. I'd feel divine inspiration, or something."

"I guess that divine inspiration came in the form of car trouble that stranded you in Pinewood," Maisie commented.

Clara grinned. "The Lord works in mysterious ways, and all that. I stayed in the motel next to the diner, met you and Josef—and Noelle—and here I am."

"I guess our situations are more similar than I thought," Maisie said.

"We're both forging new paths. And we both love to bake. Which brings me to why I'm here." Clara straightened in her chair.

Maisie raised an eyebrow.

"You don't have to decide right now," Clara continued in a rush. "Just hear what I have to say and then sleep on it. You and Josef will need to discuss."

"For heaven's sake, what're you talking about?"

"I was wondering if you'd like to become a member of my LLC? Sweets & Treats needs to have two members. It would be you and me." She looked at the older woman, whose mouth had dropped open. "You wouldn't have to do anything—or put in any money. I wouldn't expect you to work in the shop. Your advice and expertise would be your contribution. In your own time. This wouldn't be a burden…"

Maisie reached across the table and took Clara's hands into her own. "Yes."

"You should think about it."

"I don't need to think. I know in here," she lifted one hand to her heart before returning it to Clara's. "Nothing would make me happier than to be involved in your patisserie in any way that would be helpful to you." Her eyes shone.

Clara squeezed Maisie's hands.

Noelle barked as Josef opened the back door into the kitchen and hurried into the room, the delicious aroma of Italian spices and freshly baked bread preceding him. "We had lasagna as tonight's special," he began before drawing up short. His gaze went from Maisie to Clara and back again. "You two have talked?"

Both women nodded affirmatively.

Josef set the takeout bags on the counter and rubbed his hands together. "From the look of things, I'm guessing I'm in the presence of the two members of Sweets & Treats, LLC."

"You are, indeed," Maisie said.

"Let me get some glasses," he said. "I happen to have a nice Prosecco with me, just in case we had something to celebrate."

Maisie stood and went to her husband, planting a kiss on his cheek. "You knew Clara was going to ask me, didn't you?"

"We discussed it this morning," Josef said. "I told her I thought it was a capital idea."

"I see." Maisie looked at Clara.

"I'd been to see Kurt yesterday, and he told me I needed another member. I thought of… you." Clara bit her lip. A small white lie wasn't a sin. When Josef mentioned Maisie, she'd agreed that Maisie would be the better choice.

"I can't tell you what this means to me," Maisie said, accepting the glass of bubbly that Josef handed to her. "I suddenly feel like I have a purpose again."

"And I don't feel like I'm in this all alone. I can't tell you how comforting it is to know that you'll be part of this," Clara said.

"And I have to contribute more than just an occasional bit of advice," Maisie said. "I want to have some skin in the game, as they say on TV."

"Funny you should say that," Josef broke in. "I talked to Kurt this afternoon. He agrees we could give the bakery equipment to the LLC as our contribution. You won't have to buy it."

"Is that fair to you?" Clara asked.

"Kurt says we should have the equipment appraised and he'll use that to structure an appropriate profit participation," Josef said. "You'll retain voting control because you'll still be supplying most of the money."

"That sounds fair," Clara said.

Josef handed her a glass, then held his aloft. "To Clara and Maisie, the members of Sweets & Treats, LLC. May their collaboration be blessed with success and their friendship blossom."

"Hear, hear," Clara said, clinking glasses with Maisie and then Josef. They drank their toast.

"Now, let's tuck into dinner before it gets cold. And I'll do all the cleanup," he said. "I think the two of you have a lot to talk about."

CHAPTER 11

"I think you should stay here." Clara reached across the console to the back seat to hand a chew stick to Noelle. "Work on this. I won't be long."

Noelle snatched the treat from her mistress and settled onto the floor to gnaw the rawhide.

Clara was halfway up the walkway to the front door when it opened, and a woman stepped onto the porch. She was zipping herself into a puffer jacket. Her dark hair was short and styled in a simple bob. Slim and agile, she trotted down the steps, extending her hand as she came to Clara. "Laura Ramsey," she said.

Clara took her hand and introduced herself. Laura had clear blue eyes and a solid handshake. The tiny lines around her eyes told Clara that Laura was older than she was—maybe by another ten years—placing her in her early forties.

"Nice to meet you, Clara," Laura said. "Are you the one who baked those Christmas cookies we had after the Messiah?"

"I am. How do you know about them?"

"I sang in the choir and brought home the one you gave to each of us. I kept it on display for as long as I could—the piping on that cookie was like a work of art—until my son, Ian, ate it."

"I'm so pleased you enjoyed it."

"I picked up a dozen from the diner and had them for dessert on Christmas. I've got three of them hidden away for New Year's Eve." Laura grinned. "You've made quite an impression at my house. I feel like I'm meeting a celebrity."

Clara flushed with pleasure. "Hardly."

Laura started down the brick pathway that led to the guest house. "You said that you've decided to stay in town and will open a patisserie on Main Street. You want to find somewhere close by to live."

"That's right," Clara said as they walked along together. "I was exploring the neighborhood yesterday and saw the sign in your window. This location would be ideal."

"Yes. You could walk to work." She retrieved a key from her pocket. The dark mahogany front door contained an oval, etched glass window in the top half. A peaked overhang was trimmed with white gingerbread and a small porch extended to the right, allowing room for a small table and chair.

Clara sighed with pleasure. The guest house really was a miniature version of the main house. If the interior was this charming, she was going to fall hopelessly in love with it.

Laura unlocked the door and went inside, flipping on a switch to turn on a brass and glass fixture.

Clara followed her into a small central hallway. A large archway on their right opened into the living room. Three closed doors were positioned on their left. An opening at the end of the hall appeared to lead to the kitchen.

Laura led the way into the living room. The bay window at

the front provided ample daylight. A stone fireplace with an elaborately carved mantle dominated the space. The cream walls were Venetian plaster. A camel-colored leather sofa, looking broken-in but not ratty, and a large armchair upholstered in a cream and camel windowpane check provided the seating. A low coffee table and an end table positioned between the sofa and the chair were the only other pieces of furniture in the room.

Clara stepped off the walnut hardwood floors onto the thick Aubusson rug in tones of camel, teal, and coral. "This is absolutely beautiful," Clara said. "So cheerful."

"Thank you," Laura said. "There's quite a bit of color in this rug. If you don't like it, you can roll it up and I'll store it somewhere else."

"I love this rug!" Clara turned around slowly in the room. "Does the fireplace work?"

"Absolutely. It'll heat this whole place unless it's bitterly cold." She pointed to the space above the mantle. "I've got a television that I can hang there. The prior renters took the one that was there with them."

"You mean they stole it?"

Laura nodded. "Unfortunately. You have to be so careful who you rent to." She pursed her lips. "Ready to see the rest?"

"Absolutely."

They re-entered the hallway and inspected the bedrooms and the one bathroom. A deep, claw-footed tub with a shower curtain surround was fitted with a ceiling-mounted shower head.

Clara envisioned herself soaking away the day's fatigue in that tub.

The second bedroom had an oversized window that

looked onto the dormant vegetable garden along the property line.

"This window faces east," Laura said. She opened the floral drapes. "Unless you install blackout liners, this room will be very bright in the morning. Most renters opt to take the other room as their bedroom."

"I'm a baker, remember? I'll be up before four Monday through Saturday. Even on Sunday—when I'll be closed—I won't be able to sleep past five. The sun won't be a problem. I love the floral pattern on these drapes."

"We did this house up when English country house style was all the rage. I'm afraid people want a cleaner, more modern vibe now."

"This chintz is lovely in here. You've decorated this place perfectly, in keeping with the character of the house."

Laura grinned. "You're the first person in a very long time who's said that. Wait until you see the kitchen. We've kept a vintage feel, but all the fixtures and appliances are new."

The kitchen was compact, but efficient. White cabinets lined the walls and were topped with solid black granite countertops. Traditional subway tile formed the backsplash. A gas range with a stainless-steel hood was situated on the exterior wall, with a side-by-side refrigerator across from the sink. A small island, topped with butcher block, supplied needed storage and work space. A tiny square table stood in the corner, flanked on two sides by built-in seating.

"What's behind that door next to the table? Is it a pantry?" Clara asked.

"No. It goes to the smallest laundry room you've ever seen. There's a stacked washer and dryer in there. And the door to the garden."

"Can I see?"

"Of course." Laura led the way through the tiny room and out the back door. Rows of raised beds ran the width of the house, surrounded by a chain-link fence.

"Do you use these?" Clara asked, looking at the beds, overrun with leaves and detritus.

"Granny used to love working in this garden. When I was a kid, she grew enough produce to can and supply us all winter long. It's become too much for her now, and I never got the hang of it. I'm afraid I have a black thumb." She smiled ruefully. "We've let this go, but if you'd like to plant anything back here—vegetables or flowers—you'd be more than welcome. There's a spigot over there," she pointed along the back wall of the guest house, "and the fence should keep out deer and rabbits."

"I'd love to try my hand at growing herbs and vegetables," Clara said.

Laura led them back up the steps and into the house. "This kitchen is small, to be sure. For someone like you—a professional—this might not be…"

Clara raised a hand to cut her off. "This will be more than enough for me. I'll be doing all of my baking at the patisserie, and I doubt that I'll have any energy to do more than warm up take-out."

Laura's countenance eased. "So—that's it. Any questions?"

"When can I move in?"

Laura now smiled broadly. "As soon as you want. It's the twenty-eighth. How about we start your tenancy on January 1?"

"That works for me."

"You saw the rental rate and the deposit in the listing?"

"Yep. I'm fine with all of that."

"Let's go to the house and I'll fill your name in on my lease form. You can take it with you to read."

"I'll read it now, if that's okay. I'd like to sign it and get back to setting up my bakery."

They headed toward the main house.

"Let me show you where you can park," Laura said, walking to Clara's SUV. "See this part of the driveway that goes around the garage? There's parking for you behind the garage. It's covered but not enclosed."

"That'll work," Clara said.

At the sound of her mistress's voice, Noelle jumped to her feet and barked, pawing at the glass.

Laura took a step back. "You have a dog?"

"Yes. I'm sorry. I should have told you. That's Noelle. She's the sweetest little thing."

Laura bit her lip. "I'm sorry, but we don't allow dogs."

"She's housebroken, and she doesn't chew. She won't be a problem."

"Didn't you see that in our listing? We clearly state that we don't allow pets."

Clara's shoulders sagged. "I must have missed it. I can't believe this. Your guest house is perfect for me. I'd be a very good tenant. I'll take good care of the place—and I won't steal anything when I leave."

"I know you'd be great," Laura said. "Frankly, I'd enjoy someone closer to my age on the property." She hesitated, then continued. "This is my grandmother's property. I moved in here with Ian—he's my son—when my husband died. Ian was a baby, and I needed help. Granny took care of Ian while I worked. I'm a chemistry teacher at Pinewood High. Things were so easy, living here, that we stayed on. Five years ago, she had a heart attack and now needs help from us so she can stay in her own home. She didn't want to sell the place and move into assisted living. So—here we are. 'No Pets' is her hard and fast rule. She's never made an exception. Granny adores Ian, and he's longing to get a dog, but she won't even make an exception for him."

Clara brushed her hand across her eyes.

"I'm so sorry, Clara. I hope to see you around town. I'll look for the grand opening of your patisserie. You're going to be very successful."

"Thank you," Clara replied, grateful that her voice didn't crack. "I'm sorry that I wasted your time." She opened her car door as a young boy with a mop of brown hair came around the side of the main house calling, "Mom!"

"That's Ian," Laura said.

Noelle bolted from the car and raced to the lanky boy, leaping with abandon into his arms.

Ian scooped her up and pressed the wiggling body to his chest. "Who're you?" he asked, turning his chin away from her insistent licking.

"I'm sorry," Clara said. "This is Noelle." She walked to Ian and reached for her dog.

Ian dropped to his knees, then fell onto his back, wrestling playfully with the squirming animal.

"She likes you," Clara said.

Ian chuckled.

Clara bent to pull Noelle off Ian.

Laura reached out to stop her. "It's okay. Every child should have a dog. He's been asking for one since kindergarten. He's now in sixth grade. It's the one thing I regret about staying here."

Clara straightened and the two women watched the boy-dog happiness play out in front of them.

Movement from a window at the side of the house caught Clara's attention. She glimpsed a woman with a shock of gray hair staring at the scene on the driveway. Clara held up her hand and gave a slight wave before the woman dropped the curtain back into place and was hidden from view.

"Okay, Ian," Laura said. "You don't have your jacket. Let's get you back inside before you catch a cold. What did you need me for?"

"Aw…" he whined.

Clara picked up Noelle.

"That's a neat dog," Ian said, reluctant to let her go.

"Thank you," Clara said. "I'd better be going."

"Good luck, Clara," Laura said, and she and Ian walked away.

CHAPTER 12

"That's everything, then," Josef said to the appraiser. The man turned to Clara. "Did you have any questions for me?"

Clara was staring at the screen of her phone.

"Clara? Anything else?" Josef prompted.

She brought her head up sharply. "What? No. I have nothing to add. That's all the equipment that will be contributed to the LLC."

The appraiser capped his pen and put the legal pad he'd been taking notes on back into his satchel. "The appraisal should be straightforward. Some of this equipment is fairly old, but I'll be able to find comps to establish value."

"It's all in tip-top shape," Josef added.

"I can see that."

"When will your appraisal be done?"

"Tomorrow or the next day. I'll email it to Kurt and copy Clara and Maisie, as you requested."

"Thank you," Josef said, shaking the man's hand.

"It's been a pleasure."

Josef cleared his throat.

Clara tore her eyes from the screen. "Yes… Thank you for coming out on short notice and for getting your report out promptly."

"Kurt said it was important. I don't want to hold you up."

Clara and Josef walked the man out of the bakery building. Clara resumed scrolling through her screen.

"What's got your undivided attention?" Josef asked as the appraiser headed to his car.

Clara sighed heavily and peered at Josef. "I'm looking for a place to live."

"What about that guest house you talked about?"

"I saw it this morning. It was perfect! I was going to rent it, but I didn't see that the listing clearly stated they don't allow dogs." She slumped against the wall of the bakery building. "That obviously won't work for me, so I'm back to the drawing board."

"I'm sorry to hear that. Something will turn up."

"I hope so. I've been looking at listings for the past hour." She held up her phone. "So far, nothing."

"I'll leave you to it," Josef said, heading for the diner.

"Talk to you when we get the numbers," she replied, pointing toward the disappearing taillights of the appraiser's car.

Clara made her way back to her car and the waiting Noelle. "Let's drive around and see what we find," Clara told her companion. "Maybe there's another guest house near downtown that we can rent."

Clara and Noelle spent the afternoon driving slowly up and down the residential streets near the future patisserie, widening their radius of search with each pass. Clara saw no "For Rent" signs anywhere. She was about to make a second pass on the route when Noelle began to whine and fidget in the back seat.

"Need to go out, girl?" Clara pulled to an opening at the curb and walked Noelle to the tree lawn. Her phone rang as Noelle sniffed out the perfect spot to do her business.

The phone's readout showed her that Laura Ramsey was calling.

"Laura," Clara answered, her breath forming ice droplets in the frigid air.

"Hi Clara. Have you found somewhere else yet?"

"No. I've been looking all afternoon, but no luck."

"Well… if you're still interested, I'd like to offer you our guest house."

"Really?" Clara's voice squeaked with excitement. "With Noelle?"

"Yes, with Noelle."

"What changed your mind?"

"Changed my granny's mind? She saw Ian playing with Noelle. He went back inside and talked about nothing else. I also told her I thought you'd be a good, quiet, and reliable tenant. After our last bunch of renters, that carried some weight with her. The main thing was that it would make Ian happy."

"Oh, Laura," Clara fought back tears. "You don't know how happy this makes me. I just knew—the moment I glimpsed your guest house from your driveway yesterday—I was going to love the place. When I walked through it this morning, I was certain it was the place for me. For us," she said, looking at Noelle.

"I had a good feeling about you, too." Laura said.

"When can I come sign the lease? Would now work?"

"Sure—but don't feel you have to rush back over here."

"I'm only about five minutes away," Clara said. "I want to get this settled."

"I'll put the kettle on," Laura said. "You can meet my grandmother, too. She was born outside of London and always takes tea in the afternoon."

"Gosh, that sounds lovely."

"Will Noelle be with you?"

"Yes. For now, I don't have anywhere to leave her."

"Good. Ian will be thrilled. See you in a few."

* * *

"That's it then," Laura said, taking the two signed copies of the lease from Clara. "We'll take these to my grandmother for her to sign and I'll give you your copy."

"I'm excited to meet her," Clara said. "Before we go in, do you mind me asking why she's so dead set against dogs? Is she allergic or something?"

"No. Nothing like that. I'm glad you asked. You should know." Laura inhaled slowly. "When Granny was five, she was mauled by her uncle's mongrel. He wasn't a friendly dog, and they had warned her to stay away from him—but you know kids. The dog was chained up, and she got too close to him. He lunged at her, and her foot got caught in his chain."

"How awful."

"It gets worse. He bit off part of her ear and she still has scars on her neck and along her right arm. Her father heard her screaming and pulled the dog off her."

Clara's hand flew to her heart. "That must have been horribly traumatizing for her."

"It was. To this day, she's terrified of dogs. It doesn't

matter how small or cute they are. She simply can't abide them."

"I understand," Clara said. "I'll keep Noelle away from the main house and out of sight."

"Granny doesn't go outside much anymore, so I doubt she'll see either of you."

"Can I let Noelle out in the fenced garden?"

"Yes. You can't see it from the main house."

"I promise you—I'll be very careful. I don't want to do anything to hurt her."

"I know you won't," Laura said, getting up from the kitchen table where they'd gone over the paperwork. "Let's take tea into the drawing room and you can meet her." Laura poured hot water into a china teapot adorned with yellow roses. She set three matching cups on the tray.

"What can I do?" Clara asked.

"Bring that tin on the counter. It contains shortbread biscuits. We're very English with our afternoon tea."

They entered the main drawing room. Late afternoon sun cast long shadows on the rich crimson of the oriental carpet that dominated the room. A huge mirror that stretched from the mantle to the nine-foot ceiling reflected the light.

A tiny woman sat in an armchair near the bay window, looking out at the street in front of her.

Laura set the tea tray on a table positioned in the center of the window.

The older woman grasped her cane and used it to stand.

"Please—don't get up," Clara said, crossing to the woman.

The woman straightened the Hermes scarf at her neck and patted her neat white hair. "I'm Tabitha Trent," she said, shifting her cane to her left hand and extending her right to Clara.

"Clara Conway," she said, taking the proffered hand. "It's nice to meet you, Mrs. Trent."

"Tabitha, please," the old woman said. "Since we're going to be neighbors." She lowered herself back into her chair and pointed to the one opposite hers. "Laura and I are so excited you'll be with us."

Laura handed her grandmother a cup of tea with a biscuit balanced on the saucer, before fixing the same for Clara and herself.

"I understand you're opening a patisserie not far from here."

"Yes. I'm a baker and it's been my life's dream."

"It's a good dream, I think," Tabitha said. She took a bite of her biscuit. "Do you like our English shortbread?"

Clara nibbled her biscuit and narrowed her eyes, considering her answer. "Yes. I've had shortbread before, but these are different. They're very buttery—of course—but there's something else. Orange rind? Absolutely delicious. Are there cloves in here, too?"

Tabitha beamed. "You're exactly right. This is my grandmother's recipe. I make a batch every week. Those are her secret ingredients."

Clara took a bigger bite and put her hand over her mouth. "This is the best shortbread I've ever had."

"I don't know much about French pastries," Tabitha said, "but maybe I should find out."

"I'll bring you some for your tea, after my shop is up and running."

"We can trade. Shortbread for patisserie pastries," Tabitha said.

"I love that idea!" Clara said.

Tabitha took a sip of her tea.

"When you're ready, I have two copies of the lease for you to sign," Laura said.

"By all means, let's get our business done," Tabitha set her cup on the table next to her. "When are you moving in?" she asked Clara as Laura handed Tabitha the leases and a pen.

"New Year's Day," Clara said.

"Your movers will deliver on the holiday?"

"I don't have movers," Clara responded. "Everything I have is either in the back of my car or in my room at the Pinewood Springs Motel. That's where I've been staying since I arrived in Pinewood. I'm paid until New Year's Day."

Tabitha raised an eyebrow and exchanged a glance with Laura. Neither woman pursued the topic.

Tabitha handed one copy of the lease to Clara. "We're supposed to get another ice storm in the wee hours of the first. Why don't you come by tomorrow or the next day to unload your things? Ian can help you."

"You're sure—you wouldn't mind?"

"Of course I'm sure," Tabitha said. "The guest house is ready to go. I don't mind letting you move in a few days early."

Clara looked from Laura to her grandmother.

Laura looked as surprised as Clara felt. She nodded in agreement.

Tabitha continued, "I don't want you to get stranded at that motel. And they certainly won't want that dog of yours, either. You may as well bring the dog here tomorrow, too."

"I'd be most grateful," Clara said. "I'm meeting with an attorney tomorrow about the paperwork for my business, and I can't take Noelle with me. And you're right—I'm not supposed to have her at the motel. Leaving her here while I'm out would be a lifesaver."

Laura eased back into her chair as she sipped her tea and watched the happy exchange between the other two women. It had been a long time since her grandmother had had someone else to talk to besides her granddaughter and grandson. Laura's face said it all. She was clearly thrilled that Clara Conway was supplying the dog that Ian longed for, and with the apparent friendship Clara would be bringing to her grandmother. And to herself.

CHAPTER 13

"This is it," Ian said, setting an armload of paper grocery bags onto the floor.

Clara glanced at the pile of boxes and bags now nestled against the wall in the hallway of the guest house. Could that small ramshackle collection really constitute all her worldly goods? Her clothes and cosmetics were still at the motel, but they didn't account for much. She'd hastily packed up her belongings on that fateful evening when she'd discovered Travis's continuing infidelity. At the time, all she'd wanted was to take what she could fit into her car and get away from him—before he could cajole her, yet again, into believing he loved her and would change his ways. She'd heard that one too many times. Still, she'd left most of her possessions behind and made no claim on any of their joint property in the divorce filings. Was that really wise?

"Anything else you need?" Ian shifted from foot to foot. "Can I move these into the right rooms for you?"

Clara snapped out of her reverie. "No. I'll do all of that later. Thank you, Ian. You've been very helpful." She pulled her wallet out of her purse and removed a ten-dollar bill, holding it out to him.

Ian stepped back, shaking his head. "That's okay," he said. "It wasn't a big deal. If I can help with anything else, just let me know."

Clara cocked her head to one side, contemplating the responsible boy. "If you're serious about that offer, I could use help with Noelle."

A grin flashed across his face and eagerness shone in his eyes. "Sure!"

"On one condition," Clara said with mock sternness. "You'll have to allow me to pay you for your time."

"My mom says we should do stuff for other people without expecting money."

"I'll talk to her," Clara said. "I'm going to be gone a lot—working long hours, getting the patisserie set up, and then longer hours when it's open. Noelle shouldn't be left here alone all day. I'll need someone to let her out and walk her. Maybe even feed her."

"I can do that! She's a great dog. Like before and after school?" He bounced on his heels.

"Exactly. I've got a bunch of errands to run now and I will be working at the diner for the next two days to help them get ready for New Year's Eve. Noelle will be here during the day. I'll come get her before dinner. We'll spend two more nights at the motel and I'll bring the rest of my stuff here on New Year's Eve. Can you help me with her, starting today?"

"Absolutely!"

"Fabulous. I'll pay you twenty-five dollars a day. Does that seem fair?"

Ian's eyes widened. "Heck, yes."

Clara extended her hand to him, and they shook. "It's a deal. Let's go tell her."

Ian was already on his way out the back door and into the fenced garden behind the guest house.

They stepped into the crisp air to find Noelle with her nose thrust into one of the raised beds, her hind paws set and her front paws rapidly throwing dirt over her shoulders.

"Noelle," Clara cried. "STOP."

Noelle glanced over her shoulder but kept on digging.

"NOELLE!"

Noelle reluctantly turned away from the hole she was creating in the dirt and came to her mistress.

Clara dropped to one knee and ran her hand across Noelle's back. "Look at you," she scolded. "You're a complete mess." She picked at clumps of dirt and leaves that were stuck in the dog's coat.

"She sure loves to dig," Ian said, settling onto the ground.

"I can't let her track all of this inside," Clara said. She checked her watch. "You're going to make me late for the lawyer," she said to Noelle as she raked her nails through the dog's fur.

"I can take care of this," Ian said, gathering Noelle onto his lap. "I'll get her cleaned up and put her back inside. Go to your meeting."

"You're sure?"

"Yep. I'll put a water bowl down for her and I'll come back a couple of times to let her out."

"You're a lifesaver." Clara watched as Ian gently removed the debris from Noelle's fur.

The dog licked at his face, causing him to chuckle when a kiss landed.

"I've got her favorite toy in the car. It's a blue dragon with purple polka dots. It's got a squeaker in it and she can drive you nuts with it, but she loves that thing."

"Would you like your toy?" Ian cooed to Noelle.

Clara's shoulders relaxed as she watched the boy and her dog. "Be right back," she said as she hurried to her car. With any luck, she'd be on time to meet with her new attorney to discuss the LLC. Things were working out just fine.

CHAPTER 14

Clara's shadow extended long in front of her on the sidewalk as she made her way to her car. The sun on her back was warm, but the air was nippy. She quickened her pace.

The meeting with Jerry Brunk, her new lawyer, had gone well. She liked the man. He'd listened carefully to her dreams for her new business, taken notes and asked questions, and made insightful suggestions for the structure of the new LLC.

Jerry had said he would call Kurt to discuss his ideas. He'd told her he'd ask Kurt to send both of them drafts of all the paperwork and that he'd make time to review all of it right away. She'd left his office feeling like one more thing would soon be crossed off her list.

A door on her right opened and the pungent aroma of coffee flooded onto the sidewalk. Her stomach growled. The sun slipped behind a cloud and Clara shivered.

She stopped abruptly and went into the shop. She could take twenty minutes to stop for a cup of coffee and still pick up Noelle on time.

The bookshop with a large coffee bar was bustling on this late weekday afternoon.

To one side, a small case containing a picked-over selection of pastries stood in front of a chalkboard menu announcing an extensive range of coffee offerings. A half dozen small round tables, flanked by bistro chairs, were scattered in front. Patrons were lined up, six deep, waiting to order coffee. Clara joined the queue.

The bookstore took up most of the space. Clara people-watched as she inched along in the coffee queue.

A mother leaned over a young boy, insisting that he'd have to choose between the two books he was clutching. His Christmas money would only allow him to buy one of them.

Three older women were in animated conversation about a book that stood on a table with a sign proclaiming, "January Book Club Picks."

Others—of all ages and both genders—browsed through the stacks.

An acrylic display of handmade beaded jewelry stood next to the cash register. Clara couldn't keep herself from smiling. This was exactly the sort of retail shop she loved.

"Miss," the barista said to her, "are you ready to order?"

Clara turned to the young man. "Ah… Let me see." Her eyes scanned the vast menu on the chalkboard. She looked at him. "Gosh. There's a lot to choose from. What do you suggest?"

"Coffee or tea?"

"Coffee, please. Just a plain coffee."

"What's your bean preference?"

Clara furrowed her brow. "Uh…"

"What region of origin do you favor? Colombia? Hawaii? Ethiopia?"

"That's it—Ethiopia."

"Good choice. That's my favorite, too. Size?"

"As large as you've got." Clara stooped to look into the pastry case. Her choices were a blueberry muffin, a raisin scone, or a peanut butter cookie. "And I'd like one of each of these," she said, pointing to the case. She should check out the competition for her patisserie. Who knew—maybe she could supply baked goods to this coffee shop, just like she was going to do with the diner.

Clara handed the barista a twenty-dollar bill when he gave her a small paper sack with her pastries and an oversized cup of coffee. "Put the change in the tip jar," she said as she collected her purchases and made her way to the only unoccupied table.

She set the bag down and used a napkin from the dispenser on the table to wipe crumbs and coffee spills from the surface. When she was satisfied that she'd gotten it as clean as she could, she eased herself into a chair. At her patisserie, she'd make sure that the tables were wiped between every patron.

She gingerly pulled the plastic lid off her coffee, allowing billows of steam to escape the scalding liquid. It would be at least five minutes before she could take a sip without burning her mouth.

Clara removed the cookie from the bag and broke off a piece. Hard and dry, it didn't even crumble. She took a small bite, chewed, and swallowed. It was like eating cardboard. Next was the scone, which was even worse. The blueberry muffin was passable. If this was the best her competition could do, she had nothing to worry about.

She brought the coffee to her lips, took a sip, then put the cup back down. It was still far too hot to drink. Clara scrolled through her email on her phone. As before, an email from Tom stood out in the sea of foodie newsletters.

Clara hesitated for a fraction of a second, then clicked to open Tom's email. He reported that counselors were in short supply in the rural communities along the edge of the state, but that one of them could work her and Travis in during the middle of February.

Clara groaned and put her head in her hands.

An elderly woman sitting at an adjacent table, quietly reading a magazine, turned to Clara. "Are you all right, dear?"

"Yes. I'm fine. Sorry," Clara said, self-conscious that she'd drawn attention to herself. February—the *middle* of February—was so far away. She wanted to get this divorce over with.

Clara stared at the words on the screen, then scrolled to Tom's next paragraph.

"I know you want to move things along more quickly. One of the counselors here in Glenn Hills can see you both next week. I know that means you'd have to drive all the way back here for all three sessions. Still, I thought you'd like to know. Get back to me as soon as you can as to which one you want, and I'll set the appointment."

Clara drummed her fingertips on the tabletop as she weighed her options. If she waited until mid-February, she should have most of the work done to set up the patisserie. Next week was going to be very busy, what with finalizing all the LLC paperwork, not to mention the lease. She didn't want to leave town, let alone drive the four hours each way to and from Glenn Hills.

She took a long swig of the coffee that had finally cooled enough to be just uncomfortably hot. What she really didn't want was to delay her divorce proceedings by six weeks.

She drank more coffee, then tapped in her reply. She'd

come to Glenn Hills next week. Tom should make the arrangements and she'd be there. She reread the email, then punched send.

Clara rose quickly and chucked the paper bag containing the uneaten pastries into the trash. If she was going to carve out time to go to Glenn Hills next week, she'd better pick up Noelle and head back to her motel room. She'd spend the evening online, filling out permit applications and updating her to-do list.

CHAPTER 15

Clara pulled open the door to the bakery building and Maisie stumbled into her. Clara reached out her arms to steady her friend.

"I started pushing on the door and suddenly it wasn't there anymore," Maisie said, catching her breath.

"Sorry about that," Clara said. "I'd have felt terrible if you'd fallen."

"It wouldn't have been your fault if I had—just an accident. One of those things."

"Where are you off to?" Clara asked, taking in the purse slung across Maisie's shoulder. She clearly wasn't headed to the diner to grab something.

"Josef and I are going to our attorney's office to review the LLC paperwork. Kurt sent it out this morning. Did you get his email?"

Clara nodded. "I'm going to review it and talk to my attorney later this morning."

"Good. It'd be nice if we could sign everything tomorrow. I'd love to start off the new year in business together."

"Maisie." Clara tilted her head so she could look directly into the older woman's eyes. "You need to review all the paperwork carefully. Ask your attorney questions so you understand every aspect of the LLC. Then take some time to think about it. I don't want to hurry you. Next week—or the week after—is fine."

Maisie waved one hand as if to bat away Clara's concerns. "You talk as if I've never heard of an LLC before. Josef and I own several of them—for our various business interests."

Maisie chuckled at the surprised expression on Clara's face. "I'm more than just a sweet, little old lady," Maisie said. "I'm actually a pretty shrewd businesswoman."

"I wouldn't doubt it," Clara said.

"I'm more concerned that you know what you're getting into," Maisie said. "Let's talk tomorrow, after your call with your attorney. Will you be here in the morning?"

"I will. The staff needs instruction to make the cranberry lime cheesecake that's the New Year's Eve special dessert. I'm here, now, to make sure we have all the ingredients on hand."

"I watched as today's delivery was unpacked. Everything's ready and waiting. We've got enough for twenty cakes."

"Do you really think you'll sell that many?"

"We've had a sign promoting it by the hostess stand that says it's from Sweets & Treats—opening soon. It's created quite the stir. We've even taken orders for four whole cheesecakes from people who are having New Year's Day parties."

"I didn't know you did that. Smart idea!"

Maisie tapped her temple with her finger.

Clara laughed. "I think I'm very lucky to have a business partner with such acumen."

Maisie looked around Clara. Josef was standing by his car, gesturing to his wife.

"I'd better go. We don't want to keep our attorney waiting. Go make sure you've got everything you need for tomorrow."

"Thanks. I'll do that and then start in on the paperwork."

Maisie squeezed Clara's hand before she descended the short flight of steps to the parking lot and walked to Josef's car.

Clara entered the bakery, more convinced than ever that she was doing the right thing.

* * *

CLARA CLOSED the door of the industrial oven on the final six cheesecakes. She'd started earlier than usual on this New Year's Eve morning. She'd made an extra, so she'd have one to take to Tabitha, Laura, and Ian. The prospect of living in the guest house was delightful, and she wanted to thank them for bending their "no dogs allowed" rule for her and Noelle.

As soon as the cakes came out of the oven, she'd head back to her motel room to talk to her attorney. She'd reviewed the LLC documentation the prior evening and thought Kurt had gotten every detail right. She had a couple of things she wanted to clarify, but expected she'd be ready to sign this afternoon. Maisie hadn't come in yet that morning. Clara had no idea if she or Josef had any issues with the paperwork. She'd be able to tell the moment she set eyes on Maisie.

Clara occupied herself in the bakery. The diner would be busy today until it closed, early, at ten. Josef said he always wanted his staff to be off the dangerous streets and safely at home by midnight on New Year's Eve.

The other bakers were moving through their customary tasks like a marching band in formation.

"I'll mix up the next batch of rolls," Clara told one of the other bakers, carrying a large sack of flour to a commercial mixer. "You haven't sat down since I got here. Why don't you take a break?"

The woman gave Clara a grateful smile. "Thanks. I could use one."

Clara distracted herself with the familiar process, keeping her eyes on the door for Maisie.

The timer for the cheesecakes pinged, and Clara checked on them. As expected, they were perfectly baked. She propped the door open to allow them to cool. Clara stood back and admired the deep rose tops of the cakes. The sugared cranberries accentuated with thin slices of lime that she'd prepared to garnish the cakes would look lovely. Satisfied with her work, she checked her watch.

It was time to head back to the motel for her call. She'd have to wait until she returned to the diner to see Maisie and learn if they were going to go forward together.

CHAPTER 16

"You've answered all my questions," Clara said to Jerry. "Thank you for reviewing the documents so quickly."

"You're most welcome, Clara. Let me know when you open Sweets & Treats. I'd like to be one of your first customers."

"That's so nice of you. I'll be sure to invite you to our grand opening."

"I'm counting on it."

"What happens next?"

"Unless Maisie requests modifications, the documents you have are ready to sign. Kurt can handle that. He'll make the filings and you'll be in business."

"I'll be able to sign my lease and open bank accounts in the name of the business?"

"Yes—all of that. Kurt will be the attorney for the LLC, so he'll help you with any issues."

"Sounds like I'm all set."

"My very best wishes for your success here in Pinewood. We're lucky to have you."

"Happy New Year, Jerry," Clara said as she punched off the call.

She was anxious to see if Maisie was now at the diner. Clara had urged her would-be partner to take her time reviewing the documents and to think carefully about going into business with Clara, but Clara wanted an answer—a positive answer. She peered out her window at the diner. Josef's car wasn't parked in his spot. He and Maisie must not be there yet.

Clara turned back to the room that had been her makeshift home for almost two months. Clothes, toiletries, Noelle's kibble, and lots of paperwork were her only possessions that remained in the space. She needed to clear out of her room by noon and it was already eleven o'clock.

Clara moved quickly around the room, stashing her things haphazardly into her suitcase and a stack of grocery bags that she'd accumulated for the purpose. It didn't matter if things were neat and tidy—she'd be unpacking it all later that evening.

When the final armload of bags was stowed in the back of her car, Clara returned to the room to make one last pass, opening every drawer of the dresser and nightstand, and looking under the bed and in the closet. She'd collected everything that belonged to her.

She walked to the door and stood in the opening, remembering that night weeks ago when she'd crawled into that bed only hours after leaving her husband, wondering where her life would take her and cursing the car trouble that had stranded her in the small town of Pinewood.

Clara smiled as the memories of the intervening weeks

flooded her with contentment. She'd landed exactly where she belonged. She was certain of it.

* * *

CLARA PARKED in her spot behind the guest house and grabbed her suitcase and a stack of papers before heading to her door. She'd dropped Noelle off there before five and it was time to give her sweet dog a comfort break.

Her front door was unlocked, and when she went inside, Noelle didn't race to greet her. She dropped her suitcase and papers on the floor inside the door. "Noelle," she called, her voice shrill. "NOELLE."

She was running through the house when she heard nails clicking against the floor and the thunder of a small set of paws heading for her.

Clara turned in time to catch an ecstatic Noelle who had launched herself at her mistress. She was trying to calm the squirming creature when Ian joined them.

"We were outside, playing frisbee," Ian said. "She's really good at it. And she loves it."

"I had no idea," Clara said, turning her face away from Noelle's fervent kisses. She set the dog on the floor. "We've never had the chance to play."

"Just make sure you have plenty of time," he said. "She won't let you quit."

"Thank you for taking such an interest in her," Clara said.

"She's great," Ian replied. "I have nothing else to do today, so it's no problem."

"I'm glad our arrangement is working out. I'll talk to your mom about it tomorrow, if she's around—and I've got a small gift for all of you."

"We'll be home."

"Good. I've officially checked out of the motel and will be staying here tonight. I've got to go back to the diner to finish up some things, but I'll be back here after dinner. Would you be able to feed Noelle around six?"

"Sure. Where's her food?"

"It's in my car. Will you help me with the rest of my stuff, and I'll show you how much to give her?"

Together, they made short work of moving the rest of Clara's belongings into her new home. She was on her way back to the diner in under twenty minutes, while Noelle and Ian headed to the garden to resume their game of frisbee.

Clara parked next to the bakery building and was relieved to see Josef's car. She climbed the steps to the door of the bakery and took a deep breath. She wouldn't let her eagerness to close this deal with Maisie show. The older woman didn't need to feel pressure from Clara.

She walked into the room that was now a sea of tranquility compared to earlier that morning. The stainless-steel racks to the right of the door held the trays of rolls, breads, muffins, and pies that were menu staples for the diner.

The bakery staff was moving slower now, as they finished wiping down the counters and tidying the space.

Clara crossed to the racks that held her special cranberry lime cheesecakes. Some of them had already been taken to the diner. She bit her lip. She should have come back earlier to garnish them.

She was pulling out a rack when one of the bakers called to her. "We put the garnishes on all of them."

Clara gave the woman a wide smile. "Thank you! I should have tended to them myself. I lost track of time."

"No big deal. We've got you covered." The woman turned her attention back to wiping down the commercial mixer.

Clara blinked back tears. She looked at the entire crew. These women would soon be working for her. She was struck, again, by her good fortune.

"Have you seen Maisie?" Clara asked.

"She's over at the diner," one of the women replied.

Clara made her way to the door.

"Clara," called one of the other bakers. "We'll all be going home soon. See you on the second. Happy New Year."

"The same to all of you," Clara said before she headed out the door.

CHAPTER 17

Maisie waved Clara over to the booth in the corner where she sat with Josef, nursing a cup of coffee.

"Hey, you two," Clara said, sliding onto the curved bench next to Maisie. "Happy New Year."

"The same to you," Josef said. "Your cheesecake is a big hit. I expect we'll run out by the end of the night."

"I'm glad to hear it," Clara said. "I wasn't sure…"

"Enough with the cheesecake," Maisie interrupted.

Clara drew back at the unexpected outburst and raised her brows.

"Did you talk to your attorney?"

Clara nodded.

"And?"

"We both think everything's in order."

Maisie leaned toward Clara. "You're ready to sign?"

"Yes. Whenever you are. As I said, you can take your time."

Maisie rolled her eyes. "I don't need to take any more time. We've talked to our attorney. It's all there."

"Then we can make an appointment to go see Kurt next week to sign the papers," Clara said.

"Or we can sign them now." Maisie lifted a stack of papers from the bench on the other side of her and placed them on the table. "Do you want to?"

"Heck, yes!" Clara exclaimed. "I'd love to make it official right now!"

Josef chuckled and withdrew two pens from his pocket. "I was hoping you'd be needing these." He handed a pen to each of them.

Maisie pushed her coffee cup out of the way and she and Clara made their way carefully through the documents—initialing pages and signing others—making sure they didn't miss anything. When they were done, Maisie carefully placed the executed documents in a neat stack.

"I'll go call Kurt to tell him that everything's signed," Clara said.

"Before you do," Josef said, "I think this calls for a celebration."

"What do you have in mind? It's only two-thirty in the afternoon," Maisie said.

"We can toast with a glass of champagne," he said, "and follow it with a piece of that cheesecake."

"I thought you were worried about running out," Clara said.

"There are worse things," Josef said. "I can't think of a more appropriate way to celebrate the birth of Sweets & Treats, LLC. I'll be right back."

"I made an extra cake to take to my new landladies," Clara said. "You can have it for the diner."

"Nonsense," Maisie said. "Running out will increase the

sense of urgency for our products." Her eyes twinkled. "We're off to a fast start right out of the gate."

"Shall I call Kurt while we're waiting?"

"Of course," Maisie said, hurriedly sliding across the bench. "I'll just check on Josef. Give him my best."

"You don't have to leave," Clara said to Maisie's retreating back. She shook her head and made the call.

"Clara," Kurt said, and she thought she detected genuine pleasure in his voice. "What can I do for you?"

"Maisie and I have signed all the paperwork," she said. "We were very careful, and I believe we've signed everywhere we needed to."

"That was fast. I just sent out the drafts for review yesterday. Have you both gone over them with your individual attorneys?"

"We have. Everything was written up as we'd discussed." A wellspring of happy emotion and pride gathered in her throat as she said the next words. "Sweets & Treats, LLC has been born."

"Congratulations—to both of you," he said. "You're going to be wildly successful. I still need to file your articles with the corporation commission before you'll be official. I'll stop by the diner and pick them up."

"We're about to celebrate with champagne and cheesecake—today's special offering from Sweets & Treats. Can you join us?"

"Let me see."

Clara heard him rustling papers across his desk. "I have something I need to finish up for that estate I'm handling. It needs to get filed with the court today. Should only take another thirty minutes. I'll come after that."

"Perfect! We'll wait."

"No—don't hold off on my account. I won't be drinking any champagne, anyway. I still have more work to do this afternoon."

"Working late on New Year's Eve?"

"It won't be the first time. Year end is a hectic time for business attorneys. I'll pick up your signed documents and get them filed before the end of the day."

"Thank you, Kurt," Clara said. "Maisie and I are so excited about our new venture."

"Filing with the state is only a formality. Congratulations, again. I'll see you soon."

Clara stashed her phone in her purse and retrieved her mirror and lip gloss. She slashed across her lips with the gloss and attempted to secure a stubborn part of her bangs into place. She turned her face right and left, surveying her reflection before snapping the compact shut. There were bags under her eyes that no makeup could conceal, but otherwise she looked presentable.

Maisie returned to the table, followed by a server bearing a tray with three plates containing slices of cheesecake. Josef was right behind her, a bottle of champagne and three flutes in his hand.

"Veuve Clicquot?" Clara whistled softly.

"Only the best for my gals," Josef said. "I've been saving this for a special occasion. I think this is it."

"Quite right," Maisie said as he popped the cork.

Josef poured and handed around the glasses. He sat next to his wife and raised his flute. "Here's to Sweets & Treats. May it bring the happiness and success that you both so richly deserve."

They each clinked glasses with the other before taking a sip.

"This is lovely," Clara said, putting her glass on the table. "I'm so tired. I don't dare drink anymore."

"You're burning the candle at both ends, aren't you?" Maisie asked.

"I'm afraid so. I've got all my stuff in my new place—and we're not working tomorrow—so I plan to sleep in and take it easy."

"That's an excellent idea," Josef said. "Nothing bad is going to happen if you take a day off."

"Said the pot to the kettle." Maisie elbowed him gently. "What did Kurt say?"

"He's finishing up something that needs to be filed with the court. He said he'd stop by after that to pick up these," she tapped the stack of papers with her finger, "and get our LLC filed today." She checked her watch. "He should be here any minute."

"He always works like a maniac at year end," Maisie said. "I'll bet he hasn't eaten all day."

"I'll make sure we send him away with his dinner," Josef said.

"And a slice of this cheesecake?" Clara added.

"Of course."

They sat in companionable silence, enjoying the cheesecake.

Clara brought her hand to her mouth to stifle a yawn.

"Can I get you a coffee?" Josef asked.

Clara nodded. "That'd be great. Now that we've gotten the LLC set, I'm fading fast." She yawned again. "I want to be alert when Kurt gets here."

"Be right back," Josef said.

Maisie turned to Clara. "Our menu is up to you, but—

based upon the success of this cheesecake—I'm wondering if we should offer a cheesecake of the week."

"I was thinking the same thing," Clara said. "They're easy to make and store well when frozen. There are dozens of variations—and we can make them seasonal, too."

Josef put the cup of coffee in front of Clara and left the pot on the table. The two women were so engrossed in their conversation that they didn't even notice him. Josef returned to the kitchen to supervise preparations for dinner, delighted that his two favorite women were so happily engaged.

* * *

CLARA BRUSHED her hair off her face and picked up the coffeepot, pouring the last dregs into her cup.

"I'll have Josef bring you some more," Maisie said, rising from the booth. She and Clara had spent the afternoon talking about the tasks they had to accomplish to open the patisserie and sharing their thoughts and plans for its success.

Clara drank the last sip of coffee and shook her head. "I'm done. If I don't leave now, I'm going to be too tired to drive home."

Maisie peered at her closely. "You're spent. I can see that."

"I wanted to catch Kurt, but I can't keep my eyes open."

"He gets involved in something and he loses all track of time," Maisie said. Her tone held a note of reproach. "He's always been like that."

"He's a hard worker—dedicated to his clients." Clara put her coat on. "That includes us, so I guess we should be grateful."

"I know he'll be very disappointed to have missed you," Maisie said.

"Give him our paperwork—and a piece of our cheesecake. And tell him Happy New Year, from me."

Maisie hugged Clara. "Get some rest, dear. Nothing beats a good night's sleep."

Clara made her way to her car as Josef rushed over to Maisie.

"Did Clara just leave?" he asked.

His wife nodded. "She was falling asleep on her feet."

"Darn it. I was hoping those two would see each other." He sighed. "Maybe share a New Year's kiss or something."

Maisie patted him on the arm. "You're a hopeless romantic, you know that?"

"They're perfect for each other."

"I agree. We know that, but I'm not sure they do, yet."

Josef shook his head. "Those kids. Sometimes people can be so foolish."

"We're not giving up on them."

"No," Josef said, looking at her closely. "Are you tired? Do you want me to run you home?"

"Not on your life. I want to spend my New Year's Eve right here, with you."

"It's almost closing time. Why don't you wait in the booth? The staff's almost done cleaning the kitchen. We can leave soon."

Maisie parked herself in the booth and kept her eye on the parking lot. She was the first to see Kurt pull in as the last patrons went out the front door.

Josef was switching off the neon OPEN sign when Maisie reached him.

"He's here," she said. "Kurt."

Josef moved to the door and held it open. "Come on in," he called.

Kurt sprinted up the steps and into the diner. "Thank you," he said, swiveling his head around, searching the dining room.

"She left," Josef said, an accusatory tone in his voice.

"I got caught in some last-minute year-end paperwork that one of my clients needed." His shoulders sagged.

"I told her as much," Maisie said, patting him on the back. "She wanted to stay to see you, but the past week has caught up with her. I was worried she'd fall asleep at the wheel."

Kurt brought his head up sharply.

"She's fine," Maisie said. "She texted me when she got home. Here's the signed LLC paperwork," she said, handing him a large manilla envelope with the papers.

"And here's your dinner," Josef said, handing him a paper bag filled with takeout containers. "There's enough for your dinner tonight and for tomorrow, too."

"Thank you, guys," Kurt said. "You're always more than kind."

"We love you," Maisie replied. "There's also a piece of cheesecake in there for you. It's a special creation from Sweets & Treats—and it was the hit of the night. We sold out early on, but Clara insisted we save a slice for you."

Kurt flushed. "That was awfully nice. I can't wait to try it."

"Let's all get on our way," Josef said, ushering them out the door and locking it behind him.

"Happy New Year and thank you for—everything." Kurt said.

Maisie kissed Kurt's cheek and they made their way to their cars.

CHAPTER 18

Clara stretched her toes toward the foot of the bed and raised her arms over her head. She cracked one eye open. Brilliant sunshine outlined the edges of the drapes.

Noelle hopped to her feet and paced along the edge of the bed, wagging her tail and looking over her shoulder at Clara.

"Do you need to go out?" Clara pushed herself from the bed and searched for her robe.

Noelle whimpered and jumped to the floor.

"I didn't unpack it, did I?"

Clara made her way to the back door, grabbing her jacket off the stack of boxes in the hallway.

Noelle raced ahead of her.

Clara opened the door onto a cloudless morning. Noelle shot into the garden.

The ice storm had come after midnight, as predicted. Every tree was coated, and branches hung alarmingly low with the extra weight. The fence dripped icicles. An azure sun was high in the sky and the reflection off the ice amplified the light. Clara put her hand up to shield her eyes. She felt like someone had snapped a camera's flash in her face.

Clara remained just inside the doorway, her bare toes curled against the freezing cold metal of the threshold.

Noelle finished her business in a hurry and bounded inside, coming to a screeching halt in front of her food bowl.

Clara trailed slowly behind. "Hang on," she called to the dog. "I'm taking the day off and I'm not going to hurry—for anybody."

She found her shoes in the hallway where she'd left them and slipped her feet inside, making a mental note to find her slippers first thing. She scooped kibble into Noelle's bowl and set it on the floor.

Noelle tucked into her breakfast while Clara checked the time on the tiny clock on the stove. It was almost ten. Clara was shocked at how long she'd slept. She'd crawled into bed before eight and been out like a light.

Clara pulled out the eggs she'd bought the night before at the Pinewood General Store. She'd been almost too tired to stop for groceries on her way home but was glad she'd forced herself. She'd had nothing to eat—other than dog food—in her new home. Even if the supermarkets were open today, the ice storm would make the streets impassable. The offerings of fresh food in the General Store were meager. It was clear they catered to a clientele seeking alcohol or snack foods. Clara was in the market for neither of those. She'd bought eggs, butter, milk, bread, a frozen pizza, peanut butter, bananas, and a small jar of instant coffee. She had enough to sustain her if she was housebound for a day or two.

Clara found a small frying pan in the drawer below the oven and spooned a generous hunk of butter into it. While the butter melted, she inserted two slices of whole wheat bread into the toaster. She filled the kettle with water and set it to boil while she scrambled her eggs.

When everything was ready, she carried her plate and cup to the table in the corner. Noelle settled onto the bench seat next to her. Except for the instant coffee, everything was delicious.

"This is my first meal in my new home," Clara told Noelle, tearing off a crust of toast and giving it to her. "That's just to celebrate. Don't expect table food." Clara took in the scene in front of her and a wellspring of satisfaction rose in her. "I've never lived alone before."

Noelle thumped her tail on the bench.

"I mean, I know I'm not really alone." She leaned down and kissed the top of Noelle's head. "But I've never been without another human. I went from living with my mom, to my college dorm, to my first apartment with a roommate, and then to Travis." She inhaled deeply. "I think this will be good for me."

Clara took another sip of her coffee and grimaced. "This instant coffee, however, is not good for me. It's horrible. I need to buy a decent coffeepot—ASAP!" She rose and took her dishes to the sink, pouring the remaining coffee down the drain.

"Okay," she looked down at Noelle, "enough lallygagging about. We need to get unpacked."

Clara got busy moving boxes and bags from the hallway into the rooms where the contents belonged. She soon worked up a sweat and threw off her jacket. Her bedroom and bathroom items came first. She needed additional hangers for the clothes in her large suitcase that she hadn't worn since she'd arrived in Pinewood. She started a "things to buy" list and added hangers right below coffeepot and coffee.

Clara stood in the door to her room and surveyed the scene in front of her. She liked the duvet cover and matching drapes, but a pair of crisp, white shams and a few decorative pillows would be welcome accents. A coordinating bath rug and shower curtain would be nice, too. Clara amended her list.

With the bedroom and bathroom as far as she could take them, she turned to the kitchen. The bulk of what she'd brought with her would go into this room. Clara found a station on her phone that played show tunes and, energized by the upbeat melodies, was soon singing along at the top of her lungs and tearing through the boxes.

The compact kitchen contained a surprising amount of usable storage, and Clara found a spot for everything.

The final kitchen box contained her late mother's rolling pin and cookie cutters. She unwrapped them slowly, almost reverently. They reminded her of the woman who had started and encouraged her love of baking, and whose generous bequest was now making Clara's dream of owning a patisserie come true. She clutched the rolling pin to her chest. She wasn't going to put these in a drawer, out of sight. Clara found a large wicker bowl in a cabinet, lined it with a yellow and blue striped dish towel, and arranged the rolling pin and cookie cutters in the bowl. Clara placed it on the kitchen table. These items were the centerpiece of her new life.

There were now only three items remaining to be unpacked. Clara went into the living room. She removed the bath sheet she had wrapped around the carved cuckoo clock that had been a wedding present from her grandfather. She held her breath as she examined the clock. It had made the trip unscathed. She set the time and placed the clock on a hook to the right of the mantel. She attached the weights and adjusted the chains. The clock began to tick.

She next tackled the set of fine china she'd purchased at an auction with her first check as a dietician. The arched built-in bookcase on the other side of the fireplace was outfitted with grooves for plates. The richly patterned plates in Wedgwood's Florentine Turquoise pattern brought out the tones in the rug and created a stunning focal point.

Clara reached for the last item—a framed photo of her mother and herself, taken on the happy occasion of Clara's college graduation. Clara's joy and her mother's pride radiated from the print. She blinked rapidly as she set the photo in the middle of the mantel.

Clara stepped into the hallway and looked around her. Noelle came to her and stood at her side. Clara was home and, for the first time in many years, she felt at peace there.

CHAPTER 19

Clara spun on her heel and raced into the kitchen. "The cheesecake," she said to Noelle. "I forgot to take it up to the main house!" The clock on the stove told her it was almost four o'clock. She removed the treat from the refrigerator. "I need to take this to them before it gets any later."

She blew out a breath in exasperation. "I haven't showered yet today." She walked to her bathroom and regarded herself in the mirror about the sink. Her hair hung in limp hanks around her shoulders. The bags under her eyes were gone, but a blemish was blooming on her chin. She really should shower.

Noelle pawed at her leg.

"You want to go for a walk, don't you?"

Noelle wagged her tail and turned in a circle. The word "walk" was now in her vocabulary.

Clara dragged a comb through her hair and turned back to the mirror. She looked a fright. If she left the cheesecake on the front porch at the main house, she could text Laura that it was there. She wouldn't have to see anyone.

Clara and Noelle could walk around the downtown area if the ice had melted in the sunny afternoon and the sidewalks were clear. The stores would all be closed. She wouldn't run into anyone. It would be dark in an hour. If she took the time to shower and put on makeup, she'd miss the opportunity to stretch her legs.

"Okay, girl." Clara slipped her feet into the lug-soled boots she'd neatly stored in her closet. She removed her jacket from the coatrack by the door, wound her scarf around her neck, and pulled a matching knit cap down around her ears. She clipped the leash onto Noelle's collar, retrieved the cheesecake and her keys, and they headed out.

"I want you to be very quiet," she told Noelle. "Tabitha doesn't need to hear from you. We'll just leave this for them and then we'll go on our walk."

Noelle looked up at her mistress and wagged her tail.

"I'd swear you understand me," Clara said as they made their way up the steps onto the porch and left the box containing the cheesecake by the door.

Noelle didn't make a sound.

They continued to the sidewalk, where Clara paused to compose her text message to Laura. She tapped send, and they set out toward downtown.

The sun shone brightly in the cloudless sky. The streets and sidewalks were devoid of ice, but it remained in shaded spots under cars and between buildings. They walked up and down streets that Clara hadn't explored before. As expected, everyone was closed on New Year's Day. She found a shoe repair and alterations shop, a nail salon, and a coffee shop. She peered in the window of each one as they passed. The coffee shop had a glass display case in front of the menu board. The case was empty, and it was too dark to read the menu. She wondered if they offered pastries, and if they did, if they made them in house or bought them. She'd be sure to find out.

She turned the corner onto the street where her patisserie would be located. The sun was low in the sky and filled the doorways with shadows. Sweat trickled under her collar. Clara pulled off her cap. Her hair—full of static electricity—was plastered to her head.

She turned her face to the pavement to avoid staring into the setting sun, and she and Noelle walked toward the end of the block at a brisk pace. She didn't know why she was doing it—there was nothing to see that she hadn't already seen. Still, she felt drawn by the space that was the focal point of her dream.

They had almost reached the vacant space when Clara noticed the door was propped open. She quickened her pace. No one should be there on the holiday afternoon. She fished her phone out of her pocket, prepared to dial 9-1-1 if necessary.

Noelle's tail wagged furiously as they approached the door. She let out a low bark in welcome.

Kurt, dressed in jeans and an old long-sleeved t-shirt, was rolling paint onto the back wall.

Clara tugged on Noelle's leash, pulling her back. The last thing she wanted was to run into *him*. She looked like a complete mess.

Noelle barked again, this time with more volume.

Kurt looked over his shoulder, toward the door.

Clara froze for a split second, hoping he wouldn't see them.

A smile ripped across his face. "Hey, you two," he said, putting the long-handled roller into a pan at his feet.

Argh, Clara thought. There was no getting away, sight unseen, now. She clawed at a strand of dark, wavy hair that seemed to be glued to her lips. She was normally proud of her vibrant, chestnut-colored hair but when it was this dirty it looked dingy. "What're you doing here?"

"Haven't you heard? I've got a tenant who's going to be opening a patisserie in this spot. She wants the walls to be this color—Whipped Butter." He pointed to the wall behind him with his thumb.

Clara laughed. "I love it. This new tenant of yours has great taste."

"That she does." Kurt stepped closer.

Clara felt herself flush. Why hadn't she bothered to shower and pull herself together? "Seriously—I haven't signed the lease yet. This is awfully nice of you to start in on the tenant improvements."

"I'm not worried that you won't sign," he said. "Besides, I billed over sixty hours last week. I needed to do something different. Something physical. I like to paint—I find it relaxing. I know you won't be able to move in for months. I just thought it might be fun for you to see your vision board becoming a reality."

Clara ambled around the room, examining the freshly painted space.

"What do you think?"

She opened her arms and spun in a circle. "It's perfect. Absolutely perfect. I can't believe this is really happening."

Kurt grinned. "I have to paint that wall and the rest of this one, and then I'll be finished."

"It'll be too dark to paint soon."

"I've got extra shop lights in the back of my car."

"You think of everything, don't you?"

"I try."

"Can I stay and help?"

"I've only got one roller, but why don't you stay and eat with me? I ordered a pizza—extra-large. It should be here any minute and there'll be more than enough."

Clara thought of the disappointing frozen pizza that was on the menu for her dinner. She still felt self-conscious about her appearance, but she was starving.

"I'd love to. Thank you."

"Make yourselves at home," he said, picking up the roller.

"If you don't mind, I'd like to pace off the filing room and conference room spaces. I've been working on drawings of where all my kitchen equipment will go."

"Sure. We'll start construction as soon as you've settled on your layout."

"I may need to expand the kitchen out into this area." She stepped to a spot ten feet from him. "I'll need a wall of refrigerators and freezers, a bread oven with four stacked ovens, a steam pastry oven, a floor mixer, a sheeter, work tables, and storage bins. Oh—and three different sinks." She spun to him. "Are you doing all the work—yourself?"

Kurt chuckled. "Of course not. I'll hire a contractor. I've never painted a tenant's space before." He paused and glanced at her. "I wanted to do this—for you."

Clara stopped, searching for words.

A knock on the open door caused them both to turn.

"Pizza?" A young man stood in the doorway, holding a large pizza box out in front of himself.

Kurt reached for his wallet.

Clara stepped in front of him and intercepted the man.

She withdrew her wallet and handed the man a folded stack of dollar bills. "Keep the change," she said.

"But this is fifty dollars," the young man said.

"Happy New Year," Clara told him.

"Thanks! You too."

The man left and Clara put the box on the floor.

"You didn't have to do that, you know."

"I most certainly did," Clara replied. She turned and caught his eye. "This," she pointed to the walls, "is incredibly nice of you."

He shrugged to dispel the compliment. "I didn't think about drinks or napkins or plates or anything."

Clara brushed her hand along the front of her jacket. "As you can see, I'm not dressed for a formal occasion."

Kurt pointed to the paint in his hair. "Me, neither."

She opened the box. "Sausage, pepperoni, and extra cheese?"

"Is there anything else?"

"There are others I've loved in my day, but I always come back to this." She removed a slice. "May I?" She held the slice out to him, and he took it.

She helped herself and took a bite. "This is good," she said, groaning with pleasure. "They've got the spices in the sauce just right."

"I'm glad you like it."

"Noelle, leave it," she commanded as Noelle swept her nose toward the box. "I'm going to take this," she held up her pizza, "to the file room."

"Sounds good. Let me know if you need anything."

Kurt resumed painting, and Clara started pacing and making notes on her phone. They each helped themselves to more pizza and Clara asked for—and received—a measuring tape.

Kurt finished the final pass on the last wall and was sealing the paint can when Clara emerged.

"Oh, my gosh—you're finished! Already?"

"You've been back there for almost two hours."

Clara stared out the plate-glass window to the dark night beyond. "I lost all track of time."

"Do you think this will work for you? Can we accommodate the kitchen you'll need?"

"Absolutely," Clara said. "I'm certain of it. When can Maisie and I sign the lease?"

"I'll finish it up tomorrow or the next day."

"Fabulous. Let me know when it's ready and I'll coordinate with her."

"Sure." He stretched and yawned. "We'd better get out of here. I've got a new tenant, clambering to sign a lease that I need to prepare tomorrow."

Clara laughed, and she and Noelle headed for the front door.

"I'm not letting you walk home on a cold, dark night."

"We'll be fine," Clara said. "I'll be walking home from the patisserie after dark all the time."

"You won't be doing it tonight. Now that the sun's gone down, the sidewalks and streets will refreeze. It'll be treacherous out there. I can't let my new tenant injure herself and end up defaulting on the lease."

Clara laughed. "That's a bit far-fetched, but I'm sure you're right about it being slippery."

Kurt turned the lock on the front door, and they went out the back to his SUV.

"I'm not far," Clara said. She directed him the short

distance to where she lived. The curb was lined with cars on both sides of the street.

Kurt stopped in the road and peered out the windshield at the main house. "It's an old beauty, isn't it? Looks like it's well maintained."

"It is. The landlady is a grandmother and her granddaughter and great-grandson live with her. They've been so nice to me. Ian's a nice kid—he's been watching Noelle for me."

"Sounds like things are falling into place for you."

"Sometimes I want to pinch myself." She turned to him. "The guest house is a mini version of the first floor. When I get settled, I'd love for you to see it."

His face was hidden in shadow.

"If you're interested."

"I'd be interested," he replied.

A car pulled into the road behind them.

"Okay… well… I think we're blocking the road. I'd better get going." She stepped out of the car and pulled Noelle from the back seat. Clara waved to the car waiting in the street behind them.

Kurt leaned over as Clara reached to shut her door. "I'll call as soon as the lease is done. Thanks again for the pizza."

Clara flashed him a smile and gave a thumbs up before closing the door.

She didn't glance back to see that Kurt ignored the driver behind him and watched until she walked out of sight.

CHAPTER 20

Maisie and Clara stepped onto the sidewalk in front of the downtown branch of First National Bank.

"We've signed our lease and opened our bank account. What's next?" Maisie asked.

"Haven't you had enough for one day?"

"I'd like to see our new space. I've been in it, of course, when it was Kurt's law office, but I'd like to see it now."

"We've got keys," Clara said, holding up hers. "Are you sure? I don't want to wear you out."

"I am getting tired." Maisie pointed to the coffee shop across the street from the bank. "Why don't we sit and have a cup of coffee over there? I'd like to take a break and then we'll see how I feel."

The street was empty, and they crossed mid-block.

"I've never been in here, but they're supposed to have excellent coffee. I wonder if they sell pastries, too." She cut her eyes to Clara.

"I walked by yesterday when they were closed," Clara said,

"and wondered the same thing." She smiled at Maisie. "Great minds, and all that."

The coffee shop was quiet in the middle of the afternoon. They took their cups of coffee and four differently flavored muffins—the only pastries available for purchase—to a love seat positioned against the back wall. They settled themselves into the well-worn upholstery and put the muffins in front of them on an oval coffee table.

Maisie broke off a piece from the blueberry muffin and popped it into her mouth. She chewed, then made a face. "Dry as a bone," she said, reaching for her coffee cup.

Clara tasted the apple strudel and declared it to be the same.

They both sampled the lemon poppyseed and orange nut muffins and agreed they were passable.

"We should call on the owner when we get up and running," Maisie said. "Our pastries will be much better."

"For sure," Clara agreed.

They relaxed back into the love seat.

"At least the coffee is good," Maisie said. She looked at Clara. "Kurt mentioned your vision board—for this patisserie. Can I see it?"

Clara brought her hand to her forehead. "Of course! I can't believe I haven't shown it to you already. Nothing's set in stone, of course…"

"Nonsense," Maisie said. "You're in control of the menu, the recipes, how everything looks—the whole shebang. I'm just curious."

"I've got it in my car," Clara said. "Want me to go get it?"

"I'd love that!"

Clara jumped to her feet. "Be right back." Her car was parallel parked a half block down, across the street. She'd picked Maisie up before lunch and they'd gone straight to Kurt's office to sign the lease, after which they'd stopped at the bank.

She was tucking her vision board under her arm when her phone rang with a call from her divorce attorney.

"Hey, Tom," Clara said.

"I'm glad I caught you," he replied. "The counselor here in Glenn Hills can see you and Travis on Thursday at three. Does that work for you?"

"I thought she had an opening earlier in the day?"

"She did—that was the cancellation we talked about—but Travis can't make it that early. He's got patients until two forty-five. The counselor moved her other patients to accommodate you."

Clara bit her lip. Their session would be over at four and she could be back on the road by four-fifteen. She'd be home by eight thirty or nine, at the latest. It would be a long day, but she could do it.

"Clara? I hate to put you on the spot, but I'll need to confirm with her as soon as possible. If you can't make it this Thursday, she doesn't have an opening until the end of January."

"Yes," Clara blurted out. "Tell her yes. I don't want any delays in this divorce."

"Her office is over by the hospital. I'll email you the address."

"Thank you, Tom," Clara said. "I'll let you know how it goes."

"Right. And Happy New Year, Clara." He disconnected the call.

Clara plodded back to the coffee shop. Any thought—any mention—of Travis weighed her down.

Maisie was on her phone when Clara stepped back into the coffee shop.

Clara took their cups to the barista for the one refill included in their order and returned to her seat.

"She just came back," Maisie said. "I'll talk to her and text you back." She punched off the call and took the cup of steaming coffee from Clara.

"I shouldn't have a second cup, but maybe just this once? That was Josef. Kurt's contractor can meet with us about the kitchen build-out this Friday morning at seven."

A shadow passed across Clara's face.

"Josef and I have used him, too. He did the master suite addition to our house. He does great work. We'll get other bids, too," she hastily continued. "This would just get the ball rolling."

"That'd be great," Clara said. "Building the kitchen will be our most time-consuming task before we can open the patisserie. I'll be there."

"You seemed—I don't know—hesitant when I mentioned it?"

"I've got to go to Glenn Hills on Thursday—that's where I moved here from—and I won't be back until late."

"He's on another job across town. Our space is on his way and he's willing to meet with us before he goes to the other job site. Would you like to reschedule?"

"No! If he's willing to make time for us, I want to take advantage of that. I should be home by nine. I can certainly make a seven o'clock meeting the next morning."

Maisie picked up her phone. "I'll text Josef that we're on."

Clara moved their coffee cups out of the way and placed her vision board on the table.

Maisie sent her text and shoved her phone back into her

pocket. "Look at all this! You really do have concrete ideas for this business."

The two women spent the next forty minutes pouring over the board.

Maisie hovered over one piece of paper, pinned to the top. "This mockup of your logo." She traced it with her finger. "Did you design it?"

"I had the general idea. My college roommate was a graphic design major, and she did it for me. I've had it for years." Clara studied the image. The words "Sweets & Treats," in a flourishing font, sat atop a profile of a cake stand with a fluted base. A small cluster of forget-me-nots was nestled in the upper left corner. "I wonder if it's outdated. Maybe we should design something new."

"Do you like it?"

Clara stared at the image before nodding in the affirmative. "I do. What do you think of it?"

"I *love* it. So elegant and eye-catching. It suits you."

"Us," Clara added. "Let's go with it."

"Why don't we order the sign right away? It'd be good to have it in place as soon as possible."

"That's a great idea. I'm not sure how to go about ordering a sign. Will we need a permit for it?"

"I'm not sure about a permit, but we'll have to comply with zoning ordinances in terms of size and placement on the building. The sign company should know all about that. We can give Josef the design and let him run with it. He's good at this sort of thing."

"I wouldn't want to impose," Clara said.

"Nonsense. He's itching to help." Maisie grinned. "He's driving me nuts with his suggestions and questions. This would get him out of my hair."

"Then, by all means, let him at it."

"In the meantime, I'll see if they can print the logo off on a vinyl banner with the words 'Coming Soon.' We'll hang it in the window. It's never too early to get the word out."

"I like it!" Clara brought her hands to her chest. "It'll be so exciting to see my logo in a shop window."

Maisie checked her watch. "Good heavens—it's almost five. We've been talking for hours."

"No—really?" Clara confirmed the time on her phone. "Would you still like to walk through the space?"

"Not today, if you don't mind." Maisie put her purse on her arm and wobbled as she stood, steadying herself with her cane.

Clara rushed to her feet. "I'm so sorry, Maisie. I shouldn't have…"

Maisie put her hand on Clara's arm. "I won't break."

"Why don't you stay home tomorrow? I can handle everything we need for the diner."

"I'll come in late," Maisie said. "We should speak to the staff before word gets out. This is a small town—you can't keep a secret around here."

"Good point. I can't wait to talk to them."

They left the coffee shop and walked to Clara's car.

"We need to decide which items we're going to feature in the case at the diner," Maisie said.

Clara stashed the vision board in the back seat and opened the driver's side door. "I think we should start with a different item each day—maybe with a theme for the week. Like croissants—or éclairs."

"That's a wonderful idea," Maisie said. "I can just see it…"

The business partners chattered companionably about

recipes and ingredients during the short drive to Maisie's home.

"See you about eleven," Maisie said.

"Get some rest," Clara said.

"Don't you worry about me," Maisie admonished as she got out of Clara's car.

CHAPTER 21

"Questions?" Clara asked the group of bakers gathered around her and Maisie.

A sea of heads shook from side to side.

Maisie didn't try to hide her pleasure. "We're going to continue on here until the new kitchen is ready. Clara will introduce new recipes, like she did with that cranberry lime cheesecake, but everything else will be the same."

"We'll offer the same pay and benefits as you have now," Clara chimed in. "You won't have to worry about a thing."

The group of bakers Clara had come to admire smiled back at her.

"Sounds good to me," one woman said. "We all like working together." She untied her apron and pulled it off. The other bakers did the same. It was quitting time, and the crew was ready to go home.

"All right, then. I'm thrilled that you will all continue with our LLC. I'll see you tomorrow morning." Clara concluded the meeting.

Maisie raised her hand. "You'll see me tomorrow. Clara

won't be here, but we'll both be back by mid-morning on Friday."

"No worries," said one baker. "We know the routine. You can count on us."

"I know we can," Maisie replied as the bakers picked up their coats and purses from the hooks by the door and filed out.

"Gosh—that went well," Clara said when they were gone. "I think it reassured them that you're part of Sweets & Treats."

"Don't underestimate yourself," Maisie said. "They all like you. And we can trust them to get the day's baking started without us. You've got a long day ahead of you tomorrow. Glenn Hills is a good four-hour drive, isn't it?"

"About that."

"You don't need to be in here at the crack of dawn. Try to sleep in so you're fresh for the drive. And text me when you get home. I'll be worried."

"Will do." She motioned toward the office. "I brought in some recipes for us to go over—for the daily treat."

"We can talk about them over the weekend." Maisie stretched her arms over her head. "I'd like to head home, and you should make an early day of it, too."

"I need to talk to Laura," Clara admitted. "I'd like to hire Ian to help with Noelle on a regular basis, and I should clear it with her. He's been helping me already, but I'll need more of his time tomorrow while I'm gone."

"Go." Maisie opened the door and motioned for Clara to precede her. "Drive safely. And don't forget to text me when you get home."

"I promise. I'll see you Friday morning, at the patisserie."

* * *

CLARA DROVE up the driveway and was rounding the garage on her way to her parking space when Laura pulled in behind her. Clara parked and hurried to the front of the garage.

Laura was unloading grocery bags from the trunk of her car.

"Here, let me help you," Clara said, removing the remaining two bags.

"Thanks," Laura said. "I appreciate it." She led the way around the back of the house to the door that led through a mudroom and into the kitchen. "I've been meaning to catch you to thank you for that cheesecake. It was absolutely to die for. You're going to have people lined up around the block at that patisserie of yours."

They set the bags on the counter.

"I'll be able to say I knew you when."

Clara laughed. "Being a good baker won't make me a celebrity. I appreciate your confidence, though."

"How are things at the guest house? Are you comfortable? Do you need anything?"

"It's perfect. I'm loving it. I may never want to leave."

"That would suit us just fine. Especially Ian—he's besotted with that dog of yours. All he can talk about is Noelle."

"That's why I'm here," Clara said. "He's been helping me with her—letting her out, feeding her, playing with her."

"And loving every minute of it."

"I want to make it clear that I'm paying him for this…"

"Whoa," Laura said. "You don't have to do that. He's enjoying himself. I should be paying you."

"I won't hear of it. His time is as valuable as anyone else's. The fact that he loves her is a bonus."

Laura furrowed her brow.

"If I hired a dog walker or took her to doggy daycare, I'd have to pay."

"There's such a thing as doggie daycare?" Laura raised her eyebrows.

"Yep. It's all the rage in big cities."

"The trend hasn't reached Pinewood." She shook her head, an incredulous expression on her face.

"Look, Ian is a kind, thoughtful, responsible young man. I'm going to need help with Noelle and probably other things from time to time. I'd like to hire him."

"All right," Laura said, a note of pride in her voice. "As long as you really want to."

"I do," Clara reiterated. "In fact, I'm making a trip back to Glenn Hills tomorrow and won't be home until nine. I'd like Ian to give Noelle her dinner and make sure she goes outside after she eats. Can I talk to him?"

"He's at a friend's house." Laura checked her watch. "He should be home in an hour. Shall I send him down to the guest house?"

"Sure. It won't take long."

Laura walked Clara to the door. "I'm glad things are going well for you. When your schedule settles down, come over for tea with my grandmother. She's been asking about you."

"Tell her I'd love that," Clara said, meaning it. She felt like skipping as she crossed the lawn to the guest house.

CHAPTER 22

Clara cut her eyes to the sign at the side of the highway that announced Glenn Hills was one hundred miles ahead. She was making good time and, if traffic remained light, she'd arrive at the counselor's office twenty minutes early. The woman's office was near the hospital where Clara had worked, and she knew the labyrinth of streets well. She'd park in the public lot next to the counselor's office.

She changed the channel on her radio. The news station was becoming monotonous. She found a pop station that played upbeat music.

The next highway marker told her she was now sixty miles away. Her shoulders tensed. She turned up the volume.

When Clara was only twenty miles from Glenn Hills, her stomach began to churn. She took a sip of the extra-large diet cola she'd picked up before she left Pinewood. Soon, familiar landmarks came into view: the outlet mall on the outskirts of town; the farm where she bought her pumpkins each fall; the antique mall whose sign proclaimed it had "Everything You Could Ever Want."

By the time Clara pulled into the parking lot, perspiration dotted her upper lip and she felt faintly nauseous. For a fleeting moment, she thought about driving straight out of the exit on the other side and returning to Pinewood. If she turned tail and ran, she'd be letting Travis win. He couldn't do anything to hurt her anymore. She wouldn't let him. Clara forced herself to drive up and down the rows of cars until she found a spot in the far corner.

Clara snatched her purse from the seat next to her and headed to the counselor's office. Despite her brave thoughts, she didn't trust herself not to chicken out if she waited in her car.

Clara walked to the entrance of the building and was stunned to see Travis's car parked in the first row. The man had never been early to an appointment in his life.

She found the office at the end of the hall. Her hand shook as she reached for the door, and she took a deep breath to steady herself. The waiting room was decorated in soothing tones of blue and tan. The space would have been calming if Travis hadn't been pacing from one end of the room to the other.

He turned to the door as she entered and flashed her that smile that had stopped her dead in her tracks all those years ago in college. A testament to the wonders of cosmetic dentistry, it was absolutely dazzling. She'd been an awkward, studious sophomore at the time. He'd been the popular senior and quarterback of the football team. Every girl on campus wanted him. Clara couldn't believe her luck when he chose her.

"Clara," he said, rushing toward her but stopping short.

"Clara." His voice was low, and she could feel his presence. Tall, dark, and muscular—Travis was movie-star handsome. At one time, she would have fallen into his arms.

Clara turned away and sat in a molded plastic chair.

"Aren't you even going to say 'hello'?"

"Hello, Travis." She didn't look at him but pulled her phone from her purse and scrolled mindlessly through Pinterest.

"Thanks for agreeing to meet so late in the day," he said.

She didn't look up or comment.

"I guess that means you're staying over."

"No."

"Don't you have a long drive home?"

Clara shrugged.

Travis sucked air through his teeth. He spun on his heel and walked to the door. "I'll be right back."

Clara lifted her eyes to the door as it closed behind him.

The door to the inner office opened and an older man emerged. He avoided eye contact with Clara as he made his exit. He was followed by a tall slim woman, with graying brown hair.

"You must be Clara Conway?" the counselor asked. She had a calming quality to her voice. "Where's your husband?"

The outer door opened before she finished her question.

"Sorry," Travis said. "I had a call to make."

The counselor stepped to one side and motioned them into her office.

She took a seat in a wing chair on one side of the office, opposite a leather sofa and matching armchair. Travis sat at one end of the sofa, leaving room for Clara at the other. She took the armchair.

"I've reviewed the notes that you've both provided me," she

said. "Thank you for being candid. I think we've got a lot we can explore."

Travis leaned forward and put his elbows on his knees.

Clara felt herself recoil. The only thing she wanted to do was get out of there.

"Clara, you filed this divorce. Can you tell us why?"

Clara's head snapped back. "It's all right there." She pointed to the stack of papers in the folder on the counselor's knee. "Travis is a cheater. Always has been. I finally had enough of it. End of story."

"I think there might be more to that, but we'll get to it." She turned to Travis. "You say that you love your wife and want this marriage to work. Tell us what you're feeling."

Travis trained his killer smile on the woman, who smiled back at him, before turning to Clara.

Good grief, Clara thought. The counselor was being taken in by his good looks and charm. She resisted the urge to bolt out the door and listened as Travis spun his tale of apologies and regrets, affirming his profound love for Clara and vowing that he'd never stray again. She'd heard it all before. He rambled on and on. Clara looked at her watch. At least they were nearing the end of their hour.

"What do you want to say to Travis?" the woman asked.

She didn't have anything to say to him. What she wanted to do was throw something at him. The thought of the glass vase on the table to her right smacking him on the head almost made her smile. "I've heard it all before, Travis," Clara said. "I'm done."

"Why won't you give us another try?" he asked with great sincerity. "What've you got going on in this other place, that you don't want to save your marriage?" He lowered his eyes to his hands. "Have *you* found someone else?"

"Not someone else; something else," she shot back and instantly regretted it. She didn't want Travis to know what she was doing.

"Like what?" he pounced on her admission. "I want to know what you need—what will make you happy."

Clara's whole body tensed.

"I'm afraid we're out of time," the woman said. "You've both done a good job of expressing your feelings. It's an important first step. We can talk about what you each want in the future when we meet for our next session." She rose.

Clara leapt to her feet, thankful that the session was over.

Travis got to his feet more slowly.

"You can schedule your next session through my website portal. I'll see you both then." She opened the door and smiled at the next couple in the waiting room.

Clara rushed out the door, and Travis hurried to catch up with her. "Are you sure you don't want to stay in town? We could grab dinner—and you could come back to our place. We're still married, you know. I'll even sleep in the guest room if that'll make you feel better."

Clara looked at him closely. Were those tears in his eyes? She'd never seen him cry before. Could he really be sorry and willing to change this time?

Clara fidgeted with her scarf. She couldn't stay—she needed to get home to Noelle. And she had her meeting with Maisie and the contractor first thing in the morning.

"I'll see you at the next session," she said as she walked to her car at the far end of the lot.

* * *

"Did you get the tracking device attached to her car?"

"It's there."

"And I won't get into any trouble by tracking her?"

"You're on the title to the car. It's legal for you to track it."

"Good." Travis took a deep breath. "So, you'll follow her?"

"What—tonight?"

"Yes, tonight. I want to know where she lives. She wouldn't tell me."

"I charge double time for overnight work. You up for that?"

There was a long pause on the line.

"You said she talked about having to drive four hours to get back here today. If she goes home tonight, I'll know where she is. I can drive there in the morning and spend the day watching her. I'll find where she lives and where she works."

"And who she spends time with?"

"Maybe."

"When will you start?"

"I can be on the road by six."

"And that'll be cheaper than if you leave now?"

"Absolutely. You'll still get the information you want."

"Okay, then. We'll do that. And let me know as soon as you learn anything."

"Will do. I'll talk to you when I'm on my way home tomorrow."

CHAPTER 23

Clara stopped for gas before heading to the highway. Her stomach grumbled, reminding her she hadn't eaten since breakfast. She went into the small convenience store attached to the gas station. The selection of anything that would serve as a meal was slim. The hot dogs that turned on rollers under a heat lamp were desiccated and shriveled. A package of peanut butter crackers was the only thing she could find that contained even a hint of protein.

She stifled a yawn. The counseling session had been draining. Clara purchased an enormous coffee and headed back to her car. Her favorite specialty grocery was only a mile up the road. She'd stop in to pick up something decent from their deli counter and eat it in the car. The detour would only take a few minutes. She needed to eat before she headed home.

The grocery's parking lot was full when Clara pulled in. The after-work crowd would be there, grabbing ingredients for dinner or a hot meal from the extensive selection at the deli counter. She used to stop on her way home from work at least once a week.

Clara wove her way through the crowd of customers. She'd missed the convenience of this place and wondered if Pinewood offered something similar. She'd have to make a more concerted effort to explore the offerings in her new hometown.

She was approaching the deli counter when she spied a familiar face. The woman placing her order at the counter was Marilyn, her fellow dietician and closest friend at the hospital where she had worked.

Clara waited for Marilyn to finish, then called to her as she stepped aside for her order to be filled.

Marilyn looked in her direction. Instead of the enthusiastic greeting Clara expected, Marilyn turned aside.

Clara pushed her way through the other shoppers, clustered by the order window, and joined her friend.

"Marilyn—it's me, Clara." She reached out an arm to hug the woman.

Marilyn stepped back. "I know who you are." Her tone was icy.

Clara recoiled. "What's… What's wrong? Aren't you glad to see me?"

"Are you serious?"

"You're mad at me? For leaving without explanation? I contacted you repeatedly right after I left, and again at Thanksgiving and Christmas, but you never responded."

"Why would I want to hear anything you have to say?"

The room suddenly seemed cloyingly hot. Clara loosened her scarf from around her neck. "What's going on? Why are you acting like this?"

"Oh, come on, Clara. You know me. I can't stand cheaters. I've lost all respect for you."

"I don't have any idea what you're talking about."

A woman standing close to them turned and stared.

Marilyn pulled Clara into a deserted aisle. "You ran off with another man! You emptied the joint bank accounts and took off without a backward glance or so much as a word of warning. Travis was frantic!"

Clara's vision wavered. "Is that what he told you?"

"He called me, looking for you. He was out of his mind with worry. Said you hadn't left a note or anything. He'd hoped you'd confided in me, but of course you hadn't."

Clara grasped a shelf to steady herself.

"Clara," Marilyn snarled, "how could you have done that to Travis? He was worried sick about you. If you wanted to call it quits, that's one thing, but you didn't have to be so cruel about it. I thought I knew you, but I guess I didn't."

"It's not true, Marilyn. None of it is true."

"So, you didn't leave town on a moment's notice? The hospital was pretty surprised when you up and quit at the end of your family medical leave. We were shorthanded for weeks."

"I left town suddenly, but I didn't cheat on Travis. He was the one having the affair. And I didn't empty our bank accounts."

"Did you file for divorce?"

"Yes, but I didn't even ask for my share of our marital assets."

"Really? Why's that?"

"I wanted a fresh start." She looked into Marilyn's eyes. "You know me, Marilyn. You've got to believe me."

Marilyn narrowed her eyes. "I don't know what to think. I've seen Travis…"

The store intercom announced that Marilyn's order was ready at the pickup window.

"I've got to go," Marilyn said, stepping past Clara.

"Do you believe me?"

Marilyn shrugged. "Goodbye, Clara."

Clara watched as Marilyn walked away. She stood, clutching the shelf, as she replayed the conversation in her mind. Why had it surprised her? Travis was a backstabber from the word go. He never took responsibility for his actions—of course he would blame her.

A woman pushing a grocery cart called "Excuse me," rousing her from her thoughts.

She flattened herself against one side of the grocery aisle. Travis's niceness to her during the counseling session wasn't sincere. He hadn't changed from the selfish jerk she knew. It was all an act. She brought both of her hands to her temples. He'd almost fooled her—again. She'd been an idiot.

The sights and sounds of the busy store closed in on her. The only thing she wanted was to get out of there. Acid churned in her stomach, and she didn't think she could keep anything down.

Clara strode out of the store, bumping into people without stopping to offer an apology. She needed to get home: to Noelle and Pinewood and her new life with people who loved her.

CHAPTER 24

The alarm woke Clara at six the next morning, her arm draped across the furry companion nestled against her. They were in the same position that they'd fallen asleep in.

Clara had arrived home shortly before ten. She'd made herself a slice of toast and eaten a banana before she and Noelle had fallen into bed. The intuitive creature had known —as dogs always do—that Clara's heart was heavy, and she needed extra dog snuggles.

Exhausted, Clara reached a hand toward the snooze button before the events of the prior day came flooding back. Suddenly wide awake, she got up and headed for the shower. She had a busy day ahead of her. The best thing she could do for herself was concentrate on the matters at hand.

After showering, dressing, and tending to Noelle's needs, Clara set out for the patisserie. The morning was mild enough to walk the short distance, but the sun wasn't yet up, so she drove.

The first to arrive at the space, she parked in the spot at

the rear door. She went through the back, turning on lights, and was unlocking the front door when Maisie and Josef pulled to the curb. She held the door open for them.

"I haven't been in here for years," Maisie said. "Not since it was Kurt's law office. I'm so excited about what we're going to do with this place."

The morning went by in a blur of activity. Josef had brought a roll of painter's tape with him and the three of them had taped out on the floor the footprints of the banks of refrigerators, freezers, ovens, worktables, sinks, and storage bins that they would need for a working commercial kitchen.

The contractor arrived right on time.

"You'll need to take space from the retail area," he said. "There's not enough room in the file room and conference room—even when we tear down the wall between them. Expansion will cost more money."

He looked at the three people opposite him.

Clara, Maisie, and Josef nodded their understanding.

"I'm curious," the contractor said. "Why does a bakery need so many freezers?"

"We freeze all our ingredients," Clara replied.

"Like—flour? I thought flour was shelf stable."

"It is, but the temperature of ingredients used in bread—or anything that needs to rise—is a critical factor. We need to bake things at the precise moment they're done rising. If we get it wrong, the finished product is either under or over-proofed. Humidity and ambient room temperature have a profound effect on our products. I've had things overproof in the refrigerator. When that happens, we have to throw the whole batch away."

"Wow. Who knew?" he asked.

"We keep ingredients in the freezer because that's the best

way to maintain a uniform and reliable timetable for our products. Take croissants, for instance. We make the dough and the butter blocks on day one. On the next, we roll out the dough and cut and shape the croissants, which go into the refrigerator. On the third day, we put them in the proofer for the last rise and then spray them with an egg wash and bake them to sell that day. We have to know precisely when they can be baked. There's no wiggle room here. We can't just start over on baking day. It all takes too long."

"No wonder croissants cost what they do." He whistled softly. "It's all very complex."

"Wait until you taste them," Clara said. "You'll understand why we're so careful."

The contractor continued taking measurements and examining wiring, pipes, and load-bearing walls. He left by nine, followed closely by Josef.

Maisie and Clara stayed, walking around in the taped-off kitchen, mimicking the steps of their staff as they moved through their tasks. Twice, they pulled up tape and moved a table or one of the three required sinks, until they were satisfied with the imagined workflow.

"We'll have to make changes when the kitchen's built out and we're actually working in it, but I think this is a very good layout," Maisie said.

"I agree," Clara said, her eyes shining. "I'm so glad you were here to think this through with me. You raised issues I wouldn't have thought of."

Maisie beamed. "Two heads are better than one."

"Shall we head over to the bakery at the diner and make sure things are in order?" Clara asked.

"We need to do one more thing," Maisie said, walking to a

tall cylinder leaning against a wall. She'd brought it with her when she'd arrived hours earlier.

"Oh?"

Maisie pulled the vinyl banner from the cylinder and unrolled it on the floor.

They stood, shoulder to shoulder, admiring the image on the banner. The logo of Sweets & Treats, in tones of pastel green, pink, blue, and yellow, sat below the words "COMING SOON."

Clara gasped.

Maisie brought a hand up to rub Clara's back. "It's really something, isn't it? To see it all stretched out, like that."

"It certainly is." Clara's voice cracked.

"Let's get this hung up before we leave. The printer gave me heavy-duty suction cups and there are grommets in the upper corners."

The two women got busy putting the sign in the window. Neither one noticed the man, dressed in black jeans and a dark hoodie, get out of the nondescript black sedan parked across the street. He leaned against the side of his car, pointed a professional camera at the window, adjusted the lens, and snapped a series of photos.

CHAPTER 25

Clara lunged for her phone when it rang and announced that Kurt was on the line. She'd forgotten that he'd called her while she was in Glenn Hills last week. She took a deep breath and answered with as much cheer as she could muster, considering how exhausted she was.

She had spent the week working on the order of menu items to introduce at the diner, training the staff on how to make each one, and calculating the correct quantities of supplies to order. She'd been training the bakers for the past week on éclairs, but they still weren't successful with the choux pastry—something was wrong, and she couldn't put her finger on it.

"Kurt—hi."

She stepped into the office of the bakery at the diner to take Kurt's call.

"Hi Clara," he said. "Am I catching you at a bad time?"

"No. It's fine."

"I left a message last week, but you didn't return my call."

"I remember now," Clara said. "I was in Glenn Hills. I'm

sorry I forgot to call you back. What's up?" Her phone pinged with another call. She checked the screen and saw that Tom was calling. She would call him right back.

"I wanted to let you know that the gas company can extend their line into the patisserie space. You'll be able to run your bread ovens on gas."

"Oh… That is good news. Gas is much cheaper." Her phone pinged again, telling her she had a voice mail. It must be from Tom.

"I saw the sign in your window. It looks great. Your logo is very…"

Her phone buzzed, alerting her to a text message. She scrolled and opened it. Tom was asking her to call him—ASAP. Something must be amiss with her divorce. "Sorry, but I've got to go. Can I call you back?"

"No need." His tone was brisk. "I've told you everything I needed to."

He hung up, and Clara placed a call to her attorney.

"Tom? What's wrong?"

"There have been some developments," he said. "I don't want to alarm you."

Clara rolled her eyes. If there was one statement guaranteed to alarm someone, that was it. "What's going on?"

"Travis found out about the patisserie you're opening."

"How in the world did he do that?"

"Have you told any of your friends here?"

"No. No one."

Tom was silent. "He may have had you followed. It wouldn't be the first time that one spouse in a divorce has done that to the other."

"Why do you say that?"

"His attorney sent me photos showing you and another

woman hanging a banner in a large plate-glass window."

"Announcing that 'Sweet & Treats' was coming soon?"

"Yes."

Clara moaned. "Travis is a control freak. I wouldn't put it past him. What difference does that make? My patisserie has nothing to do with him."

"He's asked for an accounting," Tom said. "He wants to know where you got the money to start your business."

"Why would that matter?"

"If you used marital assets to pay for anything, he's going to claim a half interest in it."

"What!" Clara exploded. She forced herself to take a deep breath before continuing, conscious of her new employees on the other side of the office door. "I'm using the money I inherited from my mother to start this business. He isn't entitled to any part of it."

"I understand," Tom said.

"Can't we say no? Refuse his request?"

"We can, but the court is likely to allow it."

"This is utterly ridiculous," she said through clenched teeth. "Isn't there something we can do?"

"There's a lot we can do—you just haven't wanted to do it."

"What're you talking about?"

"It's time to withdraw our offer to walk away, Clara. You can't give up on your half of the marital assets."

"But I don't want any of it—I just want out. If he signs the divorce papers, we can be done with all of this."

"He's not going to sign them, Clara. I know you don't want to hear this, but we're going to have to fight him. I know guys like Travis—and his attorney—they won't stop until you push back."

"I thought..." Clara's voice trailed off.

"You wanted a clean, simple break. In my years of experience, that rarely happens." He stopped talking, allowing Clara to take this in.

"What do you recommend?" she finally asked.

"We withdraw the proposed property settlement. I'll let his attorney know that we're demanding half of the marital assets. We ask for an accounting of our own—the joint bank accounts that he's frozen, financial statements from his dental practice, his retirement accounts—the whole works."

Clara groaned. "That sounds like a lot. Won't that just cause this divorce to drag on and on?"

"I think it's the only way we're going to bring this to an end."

"How long will this delay things?"

"There's no way to tell."

Clara wanted to cry.

"There's one more thing," Tom said. "Travis's attorney called and said that the counselor has a cancellation at nine a week from Wednesday. They want to know if you're available."

Her shoulders sagged. She'd have to leave her house before five. "Doesn't Travis have patients then? He always works on Wednesday mornings. Surely he won't want to reschedule appointments."

"His attorney said he wants to meet with you then."

"Do I still have to go through with these stupid counseling sessions—now that we're going to war?"

"You've already agreed to them, Clara. The court will want to see you follow through."

"All right." Her tone was dull. "Tell them I'll be there."

"Will do. I know this is difficult, Clara. Hang in there. You'll get your divorce."

CHAPTER 26

Clara relaxed into her chair and looked at the French dip sandwich on the plate in front of her. Maisie had shooed her out of the bakery, insisting that she come to the diner and sit down for a decent meal. For days, she had eaten every meal—including breakfast, which she took bites of in between showering and dressing—on her feet while attending to one of the myriad tasks on her list. It felt good to relax.

She dipped the bread into the cup of au jus. The baguette was flaky on the outside and soft on the inside and sopped up the flavorful juice as it was supposed to do. She'd tweaked the recipe for the baguettes and was satisfied with the resulting product. Clara took a generous bite and closed her eyes, savoring the taste and texture.

She was about to take her second bite when one of her bakers stormed through the kitchen entrance and rushed to Clara's table.

"It's not right," she said, wringing her hands. "It's just not right."

Clara reluctantly set her sandwich on her plate. "The éclairs?"

The woman nodded. "The choux isn't right. We've followed all of your instructions—every single one—and we've remade the dough three times now." The woman looked like she was about to cry. "And to think we did so well this week—with a different croissant each day."

"They're absolutely exquisite," Clara agreed. "Uniform, light, and flaky. I'm very proud of all of you."

"That's just it," the woman said. "Éclairs are supposed to be easier."

Clara cast a longing glance at her uneaten sandwich, then got to her feet. They had already posted notices about next week being éclair week. The bakers needed to be able to nail this—without her help. She'd be gone on Wednesday, seeing the counselor with Travis.

"I'll come over and we'll make a new batch of dough—from the very beginning. There has to be something we're missing."

"You should finish your lunch," the woman said. "We can wait."

"It's almost time for you to go home," Clara said. "I don't mind."

"Thank you, Clara. We don't know what else to do." She picked up Clara's plate. "I'll bring this with us."

"Thanks," Clara said as she and the baker hurried out the back door on their way to the bakery, discussing the possible source of the problem as they walked.

Kurt drove into the lot and entered the diner. He nodded to the hostess and took his usual seat at the counter.

The server put a cup of coffee in front of him without his

ordering it. "Daily special?" she asked, already knowing his answer.

"French dip?"

The server nodded.

"Sure." He picked up his cup and blew across the top of the steaming liquid while he turned on his stool to scan the dining room.

"Looking for her?"

Kurt spun around to find Josef leaning against the counter, smiling at him.

"Who?"

"Don't play coy with me. Clara, of course."

Kurt rolled his eyes. "Don't start on me. The last thing I need is to get involved with someone in the middle of a divorce. It's a formula for disaster. At worst, you end up alone after they get back together with their spouse, and—at best—your heart gets broken because they're on the rebound. I don't need it." He set his lips in a line. "Besides, she's not interested in me."

"Nonsense," Josef said. "Why do you say that?"

"I talked to her recently, and it was all business. She barely gave me the time of day."

"She's been a little bit busy lately. Haven't you heard? She's opening a new business."

"Very funny."

"Seriously," Josef said. "I know you like her. Give it a chance."

"Thanks," Kurt said, patting the older man's arm. "But I know what I'm talking about. I can tell when a woman's interested in me—and Clara Conway is definitely not."

* * *

"You're here late," Josef said to Clara as he stepped into the bakery.

She was alone, drying a large mixing bowl. Clara pulled her damp hair off her neck and twisted it into a messy bun on top of her head. "We were working out a problem with the choux dough. For éclair week next week."

"Maybe this 'new item of the week' theme is too much. French patisserie is tricky. Maybe you should back off…"

Clara held up a hand. "We got it," she said. "You have to heat the water, butter, milk, and salt until they boil. You only need to get the mixture that hot for an instant—to boil off extra moisture. Somehow, that step got missed. Now that we're boiling it again, it's perfect." Her smile dissipated some of the fatigue in her eyes.

"I'm glad to hear it," he said.

She untied her apron and put it in the hamper. "What brings you here?"

"I saw the light on and thought I'd say 'hi.' I haven't really seen you since your trip to Glenn Hills."

Clara's back stiffened.

"Everything going okay—with the divorce?"

"I guess," she said. "My husband is dragging his feet. I'm so busy here," she raised her palms and gestured around herself, "that I don't have time to think about the divorce. I just want it to be done."

"No second thoughts, then?"

Clara jerked back. "NO! No way. The last thing I'd ever do would be to get back together with him."

"I just wondered," he said, "since you're going back and forth to where you used to live." If she had looked at him closely, she would have noticed the relief that lightened his expression.

"I'm only doing that because my attorney advised me it would speed things up if I voluntarily went to three counseling sessions. He said the court would like it."

She put on her coat, picked up a Styrofoam container and her purse, and they walked out the door.

"It's smart to listen to your attorney."

"I hope so."

"If you ever want to talk about your attorney or your divorce—any of it—I'm a good listener."

"I know you are," she said, leaning against him.

He put his arm around her shoulder.

"I'm too tired right now to think about any of it. All I want to do is go home, snuggle my dog, and eat the rest of this French dip from lunch." She raised the Styrofoam container.

"A good night's sleep is often the best thing you can do for yourself," he said.

Clara moved off toward her car.

"Remember what I said, Clara. I'm here for you whenever you need me."

CHAPTER 27

"You can't come with me, girl," Clara told Noelle, who stared up at her, wagging her tail a mile a minute. She dropped to one knee and let Noelle shower her with kisses. "You know, don't you? You sense that I'm nervous and dreading this trip."

Noelle nuzzled her mistress.

"I'll be fine. Don't worry about me. Knowing I've got you to come home to is all the help I need." She hugged the squirming dog to her, then stood. "Ian will let you out during the day, and I'm sure he'll play with you."

Clara put on her gloves. "You'll love that. Be a good girl."

Noelle whimpered and pawed at Clara's leg as she went out the door.

Clara checked the clock on her dashboard. She'd have time to stop for coffee before she headed to Glenn Hills for the second counseling appointment with Travis. The thought of devoting an entire day to this useless formality irritated her. Still, it had to be done, and she'd be one step closer to her divorce.

She opened her audiobook app to *The Joy of Baking—The Everyday Zen of Watching Bread Rise* by Steph Blackwell. There would be plenty of time to finish it during her round trip. She pushed play and was transported to the world she loved—the world she would now make her living in.

The miles flew by, and Clara had almost completed the book by the time she pulled into the parking lot. She reluctantly tapped pause and made her way into the counselor's waiting room.

The space was empty. Travis had not yet arrived. She checked the time. He still had a few minutes. Clara took a seat.

The inner office door opened precisely at nine o'clock. The counselor greeted Clara.

She stood and started toward the counselor's office.

"I prefer to take both of you back at once. These are to be joint sessions. I'm not speaking to either of you individually. Let's wait for Travis."

"Oh... okay," Clara said, reclaiming her seat.

"Just knock when you're both here," the counselor said, retreating into her office and shutting the door.

Clara waited. Travis was a person who was habitually late. Her mother had always said it showed his lack of respect for other people's time. As usual, her mother had hit the nail on the head.

Clara glanced at her phone again. It was a quarter after. Irritation prickled the back of her neck. If she could get up early enough to drive the four hours to arrive on time, he should be able to make the ten-minute drive from his office to be here.

She rose and began to pace. After the long drive, it felt good to stretch her legs. She didn't really want to talk with

Travis and the counselor anyway, so she should be glad that their session would be cut short.

The inner office door opened again at nine forty. "I'm afraid that we'll have to reschedule today's session," the woman said. "There's not enough time left to make any meaningful progress."

"I understand," Clara said, feeling equal parts relieved—like she was being signed out of school early—and annoyed. "I'm sorry."

"You didn't hear from your husband?"

Clara shook her head no. "Travis never contacted me."

"I'll have to charge you for today," the woman continued. "I have a strict twenty-four-hour notice policy for cancellations."

"Of course," Clara replied.

The woman stared at her.

Clara pulled a credit card out of her wallet and handed it to the woman.

Five minutes later, credit card receipt in hand, Clara returned to her car. She'd been stood up by Travis. The more she thought about it, the madder she got. He would be at his dental practice, seeing patients. He'd make up some excuse about an emergency that had kept him at the office. She could just hear him—he'd say that he'd asked his assistant to call the doctor's office and that he didn't know why she hadn't. He'd act all solicitous and sorry, when she was sure he'd intended for her to make the eight-hour round trip—for nothing.

He wasn't going to get away with this. She'd put up with his lies and manipulations long enough. She was going to his office and have it out with him. To hell with what anyone else in the office thought of her. She was going to march in there and give him a long-overdue piece of her mind.

She pulled into the parking lot of his office and was stunned to find it vacant. Not even Travis's car was there.

She got out and walked to the door. It was locked. Clara made her way along the gravel landscaping border around to a window on the side of the building. The blind was open. No lights were on, and she couldn't see anyone inside. She'd never known Travis to close his practice. Even when he wasn't in the office, his dental hygienist would be working. Something was definitely wrong.

She returned to her car and placed a call to her attorney.

"I haven't heard a thing," Tom said. "I'll call his attorney and let you know what I find out."

"What should I do now?"

"You may as well go back home. I'll call you as soon as I have any information."

Clara punched off the call and headed for Pinewood.

* * *

THE RETURN CALL from her attorney came when she was three-quarters of the way home. She'd finished listening to her book and had started in on it again, for a second time.

She answered the call on the second ring.

"Clara—it's Tom. I've got news."

"What happened?"

"Are you driving?"

"Yes. I've got about another hour before I get home."

"Would you like to call me then?"

"No. I want to hear what you have to say now."

The line was silent for a beat. "It's quite a story. Can you pull over to talk?"

Clara looked at a highway sign as it flashed by. "Yes—there's a McDonald's at the exit a mile ahead. I'll get off there."

"Perfect," he said. He didn't fill the time with small talk.

Clara steered onto the exit and into a spot in the busy McDonald's lot. She shut off her car.

"Okay. I'm stopped. What have you found out?"

"Travis was arrested late last night."

Clara gasped.

"As was his dental hygienist."

"Melanie?"

"Yes."

"Were they—together?"

Her attorney's voice was kind. "They were taken into custody at her home."

Clara conjured up a vision of Travis and Melanie shuffling to police cars, their hands shackled. She imagined an officer putting his hand on top of Travis's head, pushing him into the back of a patrol car, and Melanie's tear-stained and panic-stricken face. She pursed her lips to suppress a smile.

Clara shook her head to bring herself back to the moment. "What were they arrested for?"

"Fraud—insurance fraud—of almost three million. Sounds like they've been cooking the books over at his dental practice."

"I… I had no idea," she said.

"No one thinks you had anything to do with it," Tom said. "I talked to a detective friend. They've been investigating the two of them for years. If you'd been implicated, they would have gone after you, too."

Clara's head jerked back against her headrest. She hadn't even considered the possibility that she might have been a suspect.

"So, what does this mean? For our divorce."

"I talked to his divorce attorney. They've frozen Travis's assets. He was just arraigned and will get out on bail if he can raise the money."

"Does that include our marital assets?"

"I'm afraid it does. If he commingled any of the money he obtained fraudulently with your joint assets, they can go after them."

"We'd already taken out a second mortgage on our house to pay for new dental equipment, so there's no equity in our residence. There may not be much else."

"I'm glad you're not counting on any of it. It'll take months to untangle his financial affairs."

"As I've told you, I never wanted any of our furniture. It reflected his taste, not mine. I'm renting a furnished place for now and would rather buy new things when I eventually purchase my own house." She sucked in a breath through her teeth. "Do you think we can go back to our original offer—to let him keep everything I left behind—and finish up our divorce?"

"I would think that's a very good possibility. When I talked to his divorce attorney, he wasn't interested in discussing the accounting he'd requested from you. My guess is that Travis hasn't been paying his divorce attorney's bills—and now the expense of his criminal defense attorney will be a lot more important."

A smile played at Clara's lips.

"When it's all said and done, you might still walk away from money you're entitled to. I want you to consider that very carefully."

"I understand."

"You told me you've made all the payments on your car from your separate account."

"That's right."

"At a bare minimum, I'll want him to sign the title of your car over to you."

"I'd want that."

"Sit tight, Clara. Things are developing for Travis—and not in a good way. It may take a week or two for his divorce attorney to talk to him. He said he'd get back to me. We should allow them to make the next move."

"Okay," Clara said. "If that's what you advise. I don't want this to make things drag on even longer."

"I won't let it. Take your time and really think about whether you want to give up your rights in your marital assets. Once you sign your divorce papers, you can't change your mind."

"I will," Clara promised. "Let me know the minute you hear any more."

"Of course." He paused, then continued. "This will be in all the papers and on the evening news. Do you want me to send you links… to any of it?"

Clara was immediately sure of her response. "No. I don't need a front-row seat to his disgrace. I want to put him behind me. As soon as possible."

CHAPTER 28

Clara restarted her book before she pulled onto the highway, but she couldn't concentrate on the narrator's words. Her talk with Tom ran through her mind on a continuous loop. How long had Travis been defrauding insurance companies? And what had he been spending the money on? It certainly wasn't his dental practice since they'd taken out a second mortgage on their house to pay for his equipment and office fixtures.

His car was a Mercedes sports car—tricked out with every option available. As expensive as it was, the luxury car wouldn't account for the millions he was accused of stealing. They hadn't taken lavish vacations, and he'd never bought expensive jewelry. At least not for her.

She shut off the audiobook app. What about the property settlement in her divorce? She was entitled to half of their marital assets. Her attorney had advised her, from the very beginning, that he thought it was foolish to give everything to Travis. Would she regret walking away from her fair share? She'd worked hard during their marriage and contributed to everything with her own hard-earned money. Even though she'd inherited a sizable nest egg from her mother, she might need the money. Outfitting a commercial kitchen would be costly and the patisserie wouldn't turn a profit right away.

Her thoughts swirled, and she was amazed to see that she was already approaching the first Pinewood exit. Her guest house was further down the highway. She bit her lip, then signaled her lane change, and exited the freeway. She knew who she needed to see.

Clara drove straight to the diner. The clock on her dashboard told her it was almost three. The lunch service would be over and preparations for the dinner rush would not yet be started. She drove around to the side of the building, holding her breath.

Josef's car was in its usual spot. She sighed in relief and parked next to him. She should go straight to the bakery, to make sure everything had gone as planned without her. The staff would leave in a few minutes. If she were to catch them, now was the time. Instead, Clara got out of her car and went in search of Josef. She found him in his tiny office off the diner's kitchen.

He was bent over a sheaf of papers scattered across his desktop. He didn't hear her approach.

She stood in his doorway, waiting for him to notice her. When he remained focused on whatever was in front of him, she knocked on the doorframe.

He reluctantly tore his eyes from the papers. A smile replaced the lines of concentration on his face when he saw her.

"Clara! You're back early." He stood quickly and came around the desk, pointing her into one of the chairs in front of it. As she sat, he lowered himself into the other chair. "It didn't go too well, did it?"

"Why do you say that?" She rubbed her hands over her eyes.

"It's written all over your face."

Clara nodded. "The truth is, it didn't go at all."

Josef raised his eyebrows.

"Travis never showed up." She filled him in on what she knew.

"That's incredible," was all Josef could say. "Are you... are you upset with what's happened to him?"

Clara pursed her lips and shook her head. "I've been thinking about that. Not really. I realize I must have stopped loving him years ago. We were still married, and I was going through the motions, but he'd been unfaithful to me over and over again. If he's guilty as charged, he deserves what's coming to him."

"That makes sense."

"What I'm struggling with is the divorce settlement." She looked over at Josef.

"Do you want to talk about it?"

"You're in the middle of something," she gestured over her shoulder at his desk. "This must be a bad time."

"Nonsense," he assured her. "I've got all the time in the world." He leaned toward her. "You can tell me anything and it won't go any further—even to Maisie."

Clara smiled at him. "I don't care if she knows." Clara took a deep breath and unburdened herself.

"Let me see if I've got this right," Josef said. "You've got with you all the material possessions you want or need?"

Clara nodded.

"You understand you might be entitled to more—maybe

even considerably more—but that hanging on to get it will require a delay, maybe a long one, in your divorce proceeding."

"Yes."

"What's important to you is to end your marriage and move beyond that chapter in your life. You feel—in your gut—that you need this divorce to move on with your life."

"Exactly!" Clara sat up straighter.

"You'll be able to concentrate on the patisserie without being distracted by your divorce."

"And not just for the business," Clara said. "I want... I need to be done with Travis... so I can move on with my personal life, too."

Josef stopped himself from asking about her feelings for Kurt. Instead, he took one of her hands in his. "I think you know your own mind and you've decided what you want to do."

"I have, haven't I?" She squeezed his hand. "Thank you for taking the time to listen to me."

"Always," he said. "Voicing what you're feeling often helps solidify it in your own mind."

Clara got to her feet. "I know what I'm going to tell my attorney."

"Good," Josef said. "You'll feel better once you make that call. Before you go, would you like to see the blueprint of the new patisserie sign? That's what I was going over when you came in."

"Are you kidding?" Clara clapped her hands together and stepped to his desk.

Josef turned the papers to face them.

"What do you think?"

Clara's eyes came alive. "I think it's perfect! When will it be ready?"

"It shouldn't be long. We've got our permit."

"Will you let me know? We'll have a celebration when they install it."

"Of course."

Clara leaned over and kissed his cheek. "Thank you for being such a remarkable friend." She breezed out of his office and didn't see him blinking back tears.

CHAPTER 29

Maisie walked back inside the patisserie space. Josef had dropped her off earlier that morning after hauling in a card table, ice bucket, and ice. Maisie had set the table with an embroidered linen tablecloth she'd inherited from her grandmother. She'd polished and set four champagne flutes on the table, together with a dish of chocolate-covered strawberries. The champagne was chilling. She'd placed a dog biscuit under the table.

She picked up her phone and placed the call. "They told me they'll be done installing the sign in thirty minutes."

"It's launch time!" Josef said. He looked over his shoulder, into the dining room. "Kurt is almost done with his lunch. I'll have him there in twenty. How are you doing with Clara?"

Maisie sighed. "She isn't picking up—it's going straight to voice mail."

"Keep trying," Josef said. "We need her."

"She told me she'd be working at home all day, so I know she's around. If I have to, I can walk to her place."

"I hate to think of you doing that."

"It's not far. I'd be fine."

"Okay. Look—I've got to go. Kurt is putting his tip on the table."

Maisie chuckled. "Operation 'Get Them Together' is now underway."

* * *

KURT NODDED at Josef as he made his way to the door.

Josef motioned for him to stop and caught up with him. "Could you do me a favor?"

"Of course," Kurt said. "What do you need?"

"Maisie took the car over to the patisserie earlier and she can't get it to start. She's called roadside assistance, but she's worn out. I was wondering if you'd drop me off at the patisserie. I'll wait for roadside assistance, and you could run Maisie home."

"Sure," Kurt said. "I go right by on my way back to my office."

"Thanks," Josef said. "You're a lifesaver."

They walked to Kurt's car. "How're things going with the patisserie?" Kurt asked. "I know my construction crew is almost done."

"We'll be ready to move our equipment over as soon as the new construction is approved by the building inspector."

"I see that you've been featuring items from the patisserie in that case at the front of the diner. How's that going?"

"We sell out every day—even though we keep increasing quantities. Have you tried any of them?"

Kurt patted his stomach. "I'm afraid I have. They're delicious."

"Clara is really something," Josef said, giving Kurt a sidelong glance.

Kurt kept his eyes on the road.

"She's been a godsend for Maisie. Working with Clara has brought the sparkle back to her. She might do the same for you."

"We've talked about the problems with getting involved with someone in the middle of a divorce—if they even want a divorce, at all."

"She's getting a divorce and I don't think she'll be in the middle of it for long," Josef said.

Kurt glanced over at him. "Really?"

Josef forced himself not to grin.

"What have you heard?"

"I don't like to tell tales out of school," Josef said. "Maybe you can ask her yourself."

* * *

CLARA CLICKED off the call with her attorney and leapt out of her chair, pumping her fists in the air.

Noelle sprang to her feet and pranced around her mistress.

"He's signed the papers, Noelle! It worked out just like Tom thought. Travis has got bigger worries right now—like keeping himself out of jail. He can't afford to tussle with me over our divorce. The assets I gave up will allow him to pay for his defense lawyer's fees."

Clara scooped Noelle into her arms and danced around her living room, belting out Gloria Gaynor's "I Will Survive."

Noelle squirmed, and Clara set her down.

"Do you want to get out of here? Let's go for a W-A-L-K."

Noelle erupted into a frenzy of excitement.

Clara clipped the leash on Noelle, stuffed her arms in her jacket, and picked up her phone. She noticed on the screen what she hadn't seen when she'd finished talking to Tom: she'd missed four calls and a text from Maisie.

She opened the text as they began their walk.

Nothing wrong. Can you come to the patisserie as soon as you get this?

"We most certainly can, can't we, girl?"

Noelle looked at her mistress.

Clara took off at a brisk pace and a delighted Noelle kept up.

They went down their residential street, waited until it was safe to cross the busy main road into the downtown area, and turned onto the block with the patisserie.

Clara lifted her eyes and saw, jutting out above the door, the sign. *Her* sign. Sweets & Treats in a flourishing font, sitting on top of a profile of a fluted cake stand, with a bunch of forget-me-knots in the corner. Clara began to run.

As she approached, Kurt stepped out of the front door and looked up at the sign.

Noelle barked, and he turned to them.

Clara flung herself at Kurt, throwing her arms around him.

He brought his arms around her.

"Can you believe it?" she asked. "Isn't it perfect?" She burst into tears.

"It is," he said, not looking at the sign.

"This is the most remarkable day," she said between sobs. "Travis signed the divorce papers and it'll all be final in a few days."

Kurt drew her closer.

"And now this." She raised her face to look at the sign, tears rolling off her chin.

He brushed them aside with his thumb.

"Everything's coming together," she choked out.

Kurt smiled down at her. "I believe I said something about the start of a wonderful chapter for all of us when we stood in this very spot—on Christmas Eve."

"You did," she said, smiling up at him. "I remember." She hesitated, then stood on her tiptoes and kissed him lightly on the lips.

As Clara lowered her feet to the pavement, Kurt bent, took her fully in his arms and kissed her long and slow.

Noelle lunged at the door, breaking them apart.

They turned, Kurt's arm still around Clara's shoulder, to find Josef and Maisie huddled together, beaming at them.

"They've got champagne and strawberries for us to celebrate," Kurt said.

"The sign?" Clara asked. "How thoughtful."

Kurt raised his eyebrows at Josef.

Josef winked.

"I think this celebration might be about more than the sign," Kurt said.

"Do you think they set us up?" Clara asked, looking from Maisie to Josef and back again. She turned to Kurt, and they both laughed.

Josef uncorked the bottle, poured the champagne, and handed them each a glass.

Noelle snatched the dog biscuit from under the table.

Josef raised his glass over his head. "To the success of Sweets & Treats, to the enduring bonds of love, and to new beginnings."

THE END

Thank You for Reading!

If you enjoyed *Sweets & Treats*, I'd be grateful if you wrote a review.

Just a few lines on Amazon or Goodreads would be great. Reviews are the best gift an author can receive. They encourage us when they're good, help us improve our next book when they're not, and help other readers make informed choices when purchasing books. Goodreads reviews help readers find new books. Reviews on Amazon keep the Amazon algorithms humming and are the most helpful aide in selling books! Thank you.

To post a review on Amazon:

1. Go to the product detail page for *Sweets & Treats* on Amazon.com.

2. Click "Write a customer review" in the Customer Reviews section.

3. Write your review and click Submit.

In gratitude,
Barbara Hinske

ACKNOWLEDGMENTS

I'm blessed with the wisdom and support of many kind and generous people. I want to thank the most supportive and delightful group of champions an author could hope for:

My insightful and supportive assistant Lisa Coleman who offers exceptional editorial advice and keeps all the plates spinning;

My life coach Mat Boggs for your wisdom and guidance;

My kind and generous legal team, Kenneth Kleinberg, Esq., and Michael McCarthy—thank you for believing in my vision;

The professional "dream team" of my editors Linden Gross and Dana Lee;

Elizabeth Mackey for a beautiful cover.

ABOUT THE AUTHOR

USA Today Bestselling Author BARBARA HINSKE is an attorney and novelist. She's authored the Guiding Emily series, the mystery thriller collection "Who's There?", the Paws & Pastries series, two novellas in The Wishing Tree series, and the beloved *Rosemont Series*. Her novella *The Christmas Club* was made into a Hallmark Channel movie of the same name in 2019.

She is extremely grateful to her readers! She inherited the writing gene from her father who wrote mysteries when he retired and told her a story every night of her childhood. She and her husband share their own Rosemont with two adorable and spoiled dogs. The old house keeps her husband busy with repair projects and her happily decorating, entertaining, and gardening. She also spends a lot of time baking and—as a result—dieting.

Clara flung out her arm to stop the screeching alarm on her cell phone. She'd woken hours ago at one a.m. and her racing mind hadn't let her fall back to sleep. She was glad it was finally time to get up.

Noelle shifted onto her side and sighed heavily, burrowing her muzzle into the down-filled duvet.

Clara rolled to face the terrier/dachshund mix whom she had adopted (or was it the other way around?) and planted a kiss on the top of her head. "I know you'd love to sleep in, but bakers have to start their day at three a.m. Especially on a big day like this one. With any luck, Valentine's Day should be insanely busy for us."

She threw the covers back and padded to the bathroom, the cold tile floor on her bare feet vanquishing any remaining sleepiness. Clara turned on the water to the shower and the tiny room was soon enveloped in a thick cloud of steam.

Her thoughts raced in happy anticipation as she contemplated the promise of the day ahead. The patisserie she'd dreamed of owning since she was a girl would be ready to open by the end of the month. The beautiful Sweets & Treats sign—with the shop's name in a flourishing font sitting atop a fluted cake stand next to a bouquet of forget-me-nots—took her breath away every time she saw it jutting out over her display window. A "Coming Soon" banner in the window made her pulse quicken.

Clara had been operating her bakery since the beginning of the year from a building she'd leased from Johanson's Diner. She'd purchased all the equipment she would need from Josef and Maisie Johanson when she'd taken over the diner's bakery business. That equipment would be moved to her new location the following week. Her bakery display cases and the high-end coffee machine were already installed.

She adjusted the water temperature and stepped into the steamy shower. The hot water relaxed her muscles, stiff from the exertion of the eighteen-hour days she'd been putting in as she prepared to launch her business.

Every member of Maisie's talented baking staff had stayed on to work for her. They'd happily integrated Clara's new ideas and offerings into the items they'd been baking for the diner for many years. The dedicated "From Sweets & Treats" display case that Josef and Maisie had installed in the diner, offering a rotating array of items for sale, had been a resounding success and had garnered Clara a devoted following.

During the past week, that case had offered red velvet strawberry cupcakes, heart-shaped sugar cookies iced in an intricate filigree pattern, chocolate-covered strawberries and cherries, and Linzer hearts with raspberry jam, dusted with powdered sugar. They'd sold out of everything in the case during the breakfast rush on the first day. Even though they had increased production every day since, they were still sold out by late afternoon.

Her staff had come to her four days earlier with a genius idea. She would supply a modest amount to the case in the diner on Valentine's Day and the diner would direct customers to the new Sweets & Treats location once they'd sold out. Maisie and Josef endorsed the idea with great enthusiasm. It would be the perfect way to introduce customers to her new location. The staff had happily agreed to work double shifts the next three days to produce enough baked goods.

Clara rinsed the last of the shampoo from her hair and shut off the water. She snaked her hand through the slit in her shower curtain and grabbed her towel, rubbing her skin vigorously before wrapping her hair in the towel. She still couldn't believe her good fortune in meeting these kind and generous people who now felt like family. After mourning the death of her beloved mother and surviving the recent divorce from her cheating husband, she finally felt like the dark cloud that had clung to her had dispersed and she was living in sunshine.

Clara shrugged into her robe and padded into the kitchen to press the start button on her coffee maker. She whistled to Noelle and waited by the back door for her dog to abandon her cozy spot on the bed and make her way to the door. "Come on, girl. While we're young," she said, as her usually lively companion made her way slowly to the door.

Noelle planted her bottom at Clara's feet and looked up at her with baleful eyes.

Clara opened the back door just enough to allow Noelle to access the steps into the fenced yard. "I know it's cold, sweetheart," Clara said. "You'll have to go out there without me. I'm only wearing my robe and my hair is wet." Clara sighed in exasperation. "Go on, girl," she said firmly.

Noelle got slowly to her feet and did as she was told. Instead of tearing around the yard, sniffing out the perfect spot to do her business, she squatted at the bottom of the steps, then returned quickly to where Clara waited behind the door.

"It's not that cold out there, is it?" Clara asked, noticing Noelle's lack of enthusiasm. "Let's get you fed. I need to finish getting ready and head out." She scooped kibble into Noelle's bowl and set it in the customary spot on the floor. "I'm going to work a very long day today, so Ian will come over to let you out before and after school. He'll take you for a walk this

ENJOY THIS EXCERPT FROM SNOWFLAKES, CUPCAKES & KIT...

afternoon. I'll be home before my date tonight. Kurt's making dinner for us at his place."

Noelle stood over her bowl and picked at a piece of kibble.

Clara poured herself a mug of coffee and switched off the machine. "I have an actual date on Valentine's Day. It's been years..." Her voice trailed off as she headed to her bedroom with her steaming mug.

Clara launched into her morning routine of drying her hair and applying a minimal amount of makeup while she sipped her coffee. Her baker's uniform of black slacks, white shirt, and sturdy lace-up shoes required no decision-making. She never wore jewelry when she was working, so she didn't stop at her jewelry box. She made her bed with four swift, sure motions.

Clara hurried through the kitchen, placing her empty mug in the sink.

Noelle still stood at her bowl, gingerly eating her kibble.

Clara stopped short. "That's not like you." She went to her furry companion and knelt beside her. "Are you okay, sweetie?" She stroked the top of Noelle's head.

Noelle took the last bite of kibble and crunched it, wagging her tail.

"That's a good girl. Ian will be here by seven. I'll see you later." She gave her beloved dog one last pat before standing and heading for the front door. Clara grabbed her coat, purse, and keys from the coat rack in the tiny foyer and headed into the frigid darkness.

...from *Snowflakes, Cupcakes & Kittens*

Available at Amazon in Print, Audio, and for Kindle

The Rosemont Series

Coming to Rosemont

Weaving the Strands

Uncovering Secrets

Drawing Close

Bringing Them Home

Shelving Doubts

Restoring What Was Lost

No Matter How Far

When Dreams There Be

Novellas

The Night Train

The Christmas Club (adapted for The Hallmark Channel, 2019)

Paws & Pastries

Sweets & Treats

Snowflakes, Cupcakes & Kittens

Workout Wishes & Valentine Kisses

Wishes of Home

Novels in the Guiding Emily Series

Guiding Emily

The Unexpected Path

Over Every Hurdle

Down the Aisle

Novels in the "Who's There?!" Collection

Deadly Parcel

Final Circuit

Connect with me, please!

I'd love to hear from you. Connect with me online:
Sign up for my newsletter at
BarbaraHinske.com to receive your Free Gift,
plus Inside Scoops and Bedtime Stories.
Email me at **bhinske@gmail.com** or find me at:
Goodreads.com/BarbaraHinske
https://facebook.com/bhinske
Instagram/barbarahinskeauthor
Twitter.com/BarbaraHinske
https://www.tiktok.com/@barbarahinske
Search for **Barbara Hinske on YouTube**
for tours inside my own historic home plus tips
and tricks for busy women!

Find photos of fictional Rosemont and Westbury, adorable dogs, and things related to her books at **Pinterest.com/BarbaraHinske**

Made in United States
North Haven, CT
23 June 2024